Hairy Leg News

Hairy Leg News

Surviving Winter and Other Challenges of Balancing
Life and Work in Northern Canada

NANCY GARDINER

Copyright © 2016 Nancy Gardiner

Hairy Leg News
Copyright © 2016 by Nancy Begalki Gardiner
All Rights Reserved

Printed by CreateSpace, an Amazon company

First Edition
No part of this book may be used or reproduced in any manner whatsoever without the prior written permission of the copyright owner, except in the case of brief quotations embedded in reviews.

Names, characters, places, and incidents are used fictitiously, and any resemblance to actual persons, living or dead, events, or locales is entirely coincidental.

Library of Congress Cataloguing in Publication

Begalki Gardiner, Nancy 1956–
Hairy Leg News

ISBN 1519472943
ISBN-13: 9781519472946
Library of Congress Control Number: 2015919627
CreateSpace Independent Publishing Platform
North Charleston, South Carolina

Printed and bound in the United States

This book is dedicated to my parents, who supported my love of writing and inspired me throughout their lives. It is also dedicated to my brother, my husband and sons, JoAnn Boyer, Lynne Boyer, Valerie Robertson, Nadeen Lipari, Noreen Kyle, Jenny Fischlin, Colleen Lauzon, Leslie Croft and friends who have always supported me with love, inspiration, and humorous wisdom. I also want to take this opportunity to thank the people living in the Northwest Territories who have been very generous in sharing their friendship, knowledge, and wisdom.

Most of the inspiration for this book comes from my family and people I have met on my journey through life. I am very grateful to my family and northerners, who helped me conceive of this book.

A very special thank-you goes to NWT North Words, the NWT Arts Council, the Government of the Northwest Territories' Department of Education, Culture and Employment, and the many editors and individuals who helped to make this book possible. Thank you especially to Laurie Sarkadi, who spent a lot of her personal time to help me with this book, and to Gaines Hill for his support in getting me started on finalizing this project.

Meet the Author

When I first moved to northern Canada, I had been working as a twenty-six-year-old listings writer and fact-checker for *TV Guide* magazine in Toronto. One of my duties was contacting Hollywood publicists. While this was very unusual work, I craved adventure, and so I applied for a job in northern Canada. Northern News Services in Yellowknife, Northwest Territories, hired me as a reporter for their weekly newspaper, *News North*, at their Yellowknife, and then Inuvik, office. I later worked as a business section editor for the same newspaper. I envisioned coming north for at least six months to see if I liked it. It helped that my best friend was working at the local radio station in Yellowknife. She was the only person who I knew when I moved here.

I grew up in Montreal, Quebec, and Ottawa, Ontario. In Montreal, I first learned to relieve winter boredom by rolling snowmen and watching kids experimenting with sticking their tongues on icy railings with various bad results. I lived

Nancy Gardiner

in Montreal until I was eleven years old. About the time that Expo '67 opened, my dad, who was a Mountie, was transferred to Ottawa.

In Ottawa, the nation's capital, federal civil servants inhabiting downtown offices would joke that they rolled up the sidewalks at 5:00 p.m. when they all went home from work. I learned about year-round boredom relief with tea parties, cocktail parties, and the annual Governor General's Garden Party. The public was invited to the Governor General's Garden Party in Ottawa and given a round of food buffet-style, served on silver platters.

I did most of my education from elementary school to post-secondary in Ottawa, studied journalism at Algonquin College, and completed my bachelor's degree at Ottawa University. After working for the government in Ottawa, I moved to Toronto and worked at *TV Guide* magazine. After a year in Toronto, I moved to Yellowknife, capital of the Northwest Territories.

After a year in Yellowknife, I moved to Inuvik, where I met my husband and raised three boys. After ten years in Inuvik, we moved to Yellowknife.

While Yellowknife is around the sixty-second parallel, Inuvik is above the Arctic Circle. Yellowknife was founded in 1934 with the discovery of gold. The indigenous people were already in the area before Yellowknife was settled. It is the territorial

Hairy Leg News

government's home. When the gold mines waned, mining later focused on diamonds, which were first discovered in the 1990s.

Many of the jobs that I have held in the Northwest Territories have involved traveling on small airplanes to the majority of the thirty-three communities. My traveling jobs were with the government of the Northwest Territories' Department of Education, Department of Aboriginal Affairs, and the weekly newspaper *News North*. When I worked for the Canadian Broadcasting Corporation in Inuvik and Yellowknife, I occasionally filled in by conducting interviews, writing news stories, and assisting with research for television news. I also wrote and delivered on-air commentaries. This wide range of travel and meeting people from all over the North gave me some insight into the challenges faced by those living in remote or isolated northern communities. Some communities are fly-in only, and I was fortunate to live in communities connected to the south by a highway or ferry or bridge for visiting family or taking shopping breaks. Some of the more remote communities rely on barges to bring fuel and megaloads of groceries once a year—the only alternative to flying in groceries at ridiculous prices.

Northern Canada is sometimes referred to as the *University of the North* for seasoned winter veterans. The experience of living here for more than three decades has been a valuable informal education. This is an experience to be shared with others.

Contents

Meet the Author · vii

Chapter 1	Canadian Winters in the North· · · · · · · · · · 1
Chapter 2	Northern Seasons · · · · · · · · · · · · · · · · 32
Chapter 3	Homemaking in the Great White North · · 40
Chapter 4	Subarctic Living · · · · · · · · · · · · · · · · · 64
Chapter 5	Working North of 60°· · · · · · · · · · · · · · 78
Chapter 6	Childhood Memories· · · · · · · · · · · · · · · 98
Chapter 7	Cold-Climate Travel · · · · · · · · · · · · · · 114
Chapter 8	Boredom above the Sixty-Second
	Parallel · 144
Chapter 9	Holidays Near the Arctic Circle · · · · · · · 160
Chapter 10	Parenting in Extreme Climates· · · · · · · · 177
Chapter 11	Aging in the North · · · · · · · · · · · · · · · 194

One

CANADIAN WINTERS IN THE NORTH

I learned at a young age to appreciate dry humor. I grew up watching home movies, British sitcoms, *I Love Lucy* and *The Carol Burnett Show*. The writings of Erma Bombeck have always been my inspiration to share some of the funnier sides of life.

I have always lived in places with extreme, frozen winters. My experience in northern Canada has been a true cold-weather test on my psyche.

Southerners who come north have largely adapted to the climate and its psychological companion, cabin fever. Northerners who were born here and have lived here all of their lives understand the need to embrace the northern lifestyle for survival.

Over the years, I have observed oddities, eccentricities, and normalcies about living in the North. It has always bothered me that I have not seen an entire book about some of the quirks of living in the North and how people cope with the frigid winters. There are books on specific topics such as the ice roads, northern bush pilots, and the northern lights. However, I had not seen a book about the nitty-gritty of living in northern Canada. I decided to write about it so that people could learn about the North and come to understand a northern sense of humor.

For the more than three decades that I have lived in the Northwest Territories I have observed how people cope with the weather, sometimes loneliness, and isolation. I have also been a full participant in duct-taped snow parkas, starting campfires with sweater wool and wooden matches in frigid temperatures during Arctic-survival training, and cultivating many winter hobbies. TV and movie viewing are the strategic pillars of northern winter living.

When I first moved to Yellowknife it was -40°C solid for most of January and February with almost no snow. With global warming, January normally hovers in the -20°C to -30°C range. Snowfalls have increased even though our area is considered a northern desert climate with little precipitation. To stay warm we have central heating and some hardy northerners burn wood and pellet stoves. There's a saying up here that "there's no sweat in the Arctic."

One aspect of living in Yellowknife that requires adjustment is its high latitude. Daylight can vary from five hours in December to twenty hours per day in June. Many of us do not sleep very much in the summer.

In small northern towns such as Yellowknife and Inuvik in the Northwest Territories, people seem to be connected to each other through relatives, people they have worked with, or old friends. In some ways it is like living in a fish bowl or similar to living on a military base. In the North, almost everyone knows someone who knows you.

This book is intended to examine living in the North to see how creatively people cope with the weather and what they do to survive the isolation and winter blahs. The book is called *Hairy Leg News* because that has always been my signoff on e-mails from the North that I send to friends.

What It Means to Be Canadian in Winter

When I think of the Canadian identity, several things spring to mind: hockey, hockey, hockey, donuts, maple syrup on snow-covered popsicle sticks, and Mounties on snow machines. Hockey is the first thing that unites this country with franchise donut holes being a close second. In winter, snow removal is a regular pastime and it brings out the comraderie in all of us.

Snow Removal

In January there was a sandwich-board sign posted on the lawns guarding the cul-de-sac: "Snow removal tonight at midnight. No parking on this block or vehicles will be towed." No parking means the neighborhood is preparing for another sleepless night of *beep, beep* from the plows and their backup warnings, which leave people wondering why they don't plow during the daytime. Hardly anybody is home during the daytime in suburbia as just about everyone works. The snowplow and grader drivers do deserve exceptional credit for working all night in the cold and dark. It takes a special person to be able to work that shift and deal with the bleakness.

At about 2:40 a.m., I woke in the back bedroom to the imagined sounds of two triceratops in heat charging each other from a block away, and then *beep-beeping* as they backed up to charge again. It was the graders. They were scraping the snow right down to the pavement, the sound like metal grinding on metal against the background roar of heavy machinery.

Another sleepless night in another cold Canadian winter.

Hairy Leg News

By 4:00 a.m. *Beep, beep!* "Hey, mistah!" *Beep, beep!*——the graders had made a four-foot-high snowbank down the middle of the road, the hardpack snow like white pyramid chunks. Mini cliffs stood at the end of driveways, where the machines took the snow down to the pavement of roads and sidewalks. Should a driver roll off one of those cliffs the next morning, the fall would be like driving off the hoist during an oil change. It might take a bit more driveway shoveling on our part for that not to happen.

Sometimes the grader leaves nice big snowbanks at the end of the driveway. If you live in a cul-de-sac, it might take the grader a week to find you. When they do come by, it's usually after you've already shoveled your driveway.

There are techniques for dealing with the two-foot-high grader ridge left at the end of the driveway. People can choose to shovel the snow, or they can rev up their engines and try smashing through it with their cars as they're now late for work.

Blasting through is more fun, but it can leave people stuck. Then the shovel comes out. There is the rocking back and forth of the car. Then the neighbors start noticing smoke, fumes, loud noises, and cursing and wander over to help push you out amid lots of kibitzing. They are helpful, with instructions like, "Try putting it in neutral while we push" and "Yeah, none of your wheels are touching the ground. Your car is entirely centered on snow." Or the neighbors will come by with an assortment of chains to hook up to a pickup truck to pull you out. These neighbors are the best! People driving by give you "the grin." It's the grin that says, "I know what you're going through because we just got out of our driveway the same way."

One morning, after we'd finally extracted the car like a bad molar, all I wanted to do was roll back onto my driveway, go into my house, make a strong coffee, and go back to bed. But, no, I had to make it to work, and now I was late. To top it off, there were no more parking spots left near work, which left the choice of parking in a snowbank and possibly getting stuck again or parking in Siberia and walking in -57°C for ten blocks. And if they were also plowing the downtown area, parking would be twenty blocks away, so it was better to walk from home to work.

If you ended up walking, your hands, even though they were in gloves, would be frozen blocks. Your eyelashes would be coated in ice crystals; sensitive cold teeth would start to complain, and you would know you would be shivering for the rest of the day. It's nothing a good shot of brandy wouldn't cure, but you'd be at work so you'd settle for a cup of coffee. By the end of the day, you'd walk ten blocks back to your car, warm it up for fifteen minutes, drive home, and then gun it up your driveway. Or you could choose to park out front, shovel the driveway, and then gun it up the driveway.

If you have a steep driveway like we do, you know what it's like trying to walk up or down the driveway on black ice. Some people know what a broken leg feels like after walking down an icy driveway. In winter, people with steep driveways clutch anything along the way to the road—the light pole, the fence, or the shovel. Some savvy individuals buy the spike attachments for their boot bottoms to walk on ice, or they use canes with spikes that pop out like a James Bond movie weapon. One day I heard on the news that an elderly lady was attacked by a young man, and she got him with the spiked cane in the groin area. That was one spunky lady. Needless to say, she did not get robbed and was fine. The robber, not so fine.

The leaf blower is another method used for the removal of snow when it is light, fluffy snow. I have seen our neighbor Fred use the leaf blower to clear off his sidewalks, driveway and truck. This is an excellent demonstration of the creativity used by northerners to deal with snowfalls.

Muscle Bag and Snowblower

There are some benefits to living in Canada in the wintertime. One is the snow outside. For example, one day while warming up a muscle-pain relief bag, I accidentally punched ten minutes instead of one minute on the microwave oven. While pulling the bag out of the microwave I discovered a big smoking hole in the center. So I ran with the smoldering bag to the front door and tossed it into the snowbank, where it fizzled and twizzled down into the snow like the melting witch from *The Wizard of Oz*.

On another day my husband was out with the snowblower doing the driveway and walkway. He hit something with the blower, and all these pieces of purple cloth went *pfffffutttt* into the air. He asked what that could have been. I responded, "Oh, that must have been the muscle-warming bag."

Pffffuttt!

Cold, Wet Snow

Shoveling cold, wet snow is a lot different than shoveling the fluffy stuff. For one thing, the snow is heavier. It also sticks to the shovel. My neighbor Sally offered a tip of the day to spray the shovel with cooking oil. I have never tried that, figuring the aerosol spray of the cooking oil in -40°C would just create—more snow.

For those completely bored by winter, some people have tried boiling water and throwing it into the air. The temperature has to be -20°C or colder. This procedure makes frozen ice crystals or snowflakes, which seems ingenious.

There is no need to go to the gym for a workout. Shoveling concrete-hard snow is a good physical under-taking, and it is a major pastime in winter. Shovels are set into snowbanks in sequential precision, small to bigger, like weapons of mass destruction. The downside of heavy snow is that grizzled winter veterans can't drive at fast speeds so that the snow can fly off their car windshields.

Snowstorms

Snowstorms create many inconveniences, including power outages, cars rocking on ice, and air-travel disruptions and delays. They also wreak havoc on roadways. I am a firm be-liever in staying put if at all possible.

Weather Reports Are Highly Exaggerated

The other day the weather forecast was -16°C and balmy. Reality: gale-force winds spun weather vanes so strong-ly that the roosters were launched into snowbanks, and a loose-garbage vortex erupted out of pickup trucks. We refer to these forecasts as weather "predictions."

Light snow traveled fast along the road tops like spirits commiserating on ice. The snow streaked horizontally, and the clouds sped past the moon at hyper speed. It was morning and dark. A neighbor checked her mail and called her dogs back. I was amazed she could open her mailbox, as mine was frozen shut with ice and snow. She was wearing the full-snow goose-down parka, hood up, and I couldn't see her face. All I heard was her voice.

When it was -57°C with high-velocity winds, it was reported that an empty hot tub had been spotted careening down the street like a toboggan. Had it been full of hot water, several locals would have jumped in, parkas and all. The drive-thru window attendants in Yellowknife thought it hilarious that individuals kept ordering iced coffees and ice cream when temperatures were in the plunging minuses.

High-Wind Explanations

Last night and this morning, we clocked ninety-kilometer winds, which explains:

a) why our garbage can lid and barbecue cover flew with a gust into my neighbor's backyard this morning;

b) why the ravens' feathers were looking like Rod Stewart's spiked hair; and

c) why there were no kids at the bus stop this morning. They either got rides or gave up on waiting for the bus.

Snow and Amplification of Sound

People can hear a feather drop from a block away when there are three feet of snow on the lawn. The snow amplifies sound. For instance, at the outdoor hockey rink down yonder, the players are discussing the style of NHL hockey player P. K. Subban. It reminds folks when talking on their cell phones outside to whisper. At the bus stop, one kid was relating how his grandmother had thirteen children. In one-upmanship, another kid said his granny had thirty-two children. The bus stop is a quarter mile from my driveway.

Shortages in Winter

Northerners are used to wintertime supply shortages. Our winters in Yellowknife start around the end of September and may continue into May. Around Thanksgiving we can start running out of pumpkin-pie filling. By Christmastime, there may be butter and pie-shell shortages. There can also be a depletion of bread, milk, and gas supplies when northern ferries stop running due to spring break up and freeze up. There is a time lag until the water freezes and the waterways can become ice roads. At Eastertime there may be a shortage of frozen bread and fresh hot cross buns. This always calls for some magical planning when stocking the pantry and freezer. In the summertime, during forest-fire season, we may run short on jet fuel, gas, ham, chicken, and bread.

In the more remote communities, a place can go for weeks without nail polish, bobby pins, egg-roll wrappers, plant soil, decent bananas and tomatoes, garlic buds, mud masks, cake decorations—especially double-digit birthday numbers—and fine dental floss. In Inuvik, there were bra-size shortages and diapers-bigger-than-eighteen-month-size shortages. If the Mad Trapper of Rat River had been a woman, he probably would have lost it when he discovered there were no more emery boards in town.

Floatplanes

Another winter oddity is that the floatplanes wear their "winter tires"—skis—and land on the plowed ice of the big lake. Someone lines the ice-road runway with Christmas trees to make it more visible to pilots. Then someone else decorates the trees with empty pop cans. That is a northern sense of humor in a nutshell.

Northern Freezer

Our version of the northern freezer has been this: place the freezer outside the house and do not plug it in all winter.

Bring frozen ham and bacon into the house. With fogged-up eyeglasses, glide across the kitchen floor to the fridge on frozen boots and start cooking!

Flight of the Giant Bumblebees

While I was doing laundry in the basement, the sounds of giant bumblebees rumbled the ground next door. It was the neighbors' kids, roaring in on their snow machines for Christmas.

Here in the North, we handle snow machines the way southerners drive cars. People like buzzing down the right sides of the roads. The only rules of thumb are to wear a helmet, don't get stuck or run out of gas, and don't fall off.

Packing survival gear is another essential. Northerners like blitzing down the ice roads on snow machines or riding over hill and dale. These machines are great for roaming into the bush in search of a Christmas tree. An elder once told me that the snow machine had replaced dog teams but that "you can't eat snow machines if you're lost in the bush." She was a very wise elder.

Sticking to Things

In the cold weather, there is an adhesive quality to objects and ice. For instance, ceramic coffee cups, scarves, and leather coats stick to frosty metal railings or frozen door handles like Velcro. The best remedies are to drink coffee indoors and stay home.

Postal Boxes

Our community postal box sits in the cul-de-sac all winter, and it has weathered the worst conditions imaginable. It is now near the end of winter, and the key does not work in the locked box. I am not sure if the entire postal box shifted in the cold. It will take about a week to get a new lock and key. I wonder what is in there. If it is bills and flyers then we are not in a hurry to get the lock fixed. Some days it is so cold that we drive from our homes to the mailboxes even though they are one hundred feet away from our houses.

Winter Tourism

A scan of Canadian winter attractions for tourists reveals a variety pack of excitement. Inuvik is trying to increase its winter tourism traffic, and Quebec City has a major attraction, the ice hotel. Yellowknife and other northern areas have aurora borealis, aka northern lights, which are a big attraction for overseas tourists. Other places have Winterlude, winter solstice, and ice palaces.

Our own version of the ice hotel is when the power goes out, the furnace grinds to a halt, and we wake up with the floors freezing cold. Then we have to worry about the pipes bursting, and we hope that never happens on a Sunday. Trying to get a plumber on his or her day off in a remote place is like trying to finagle an invitation to the Queen's garden party.

Northern Lights

There is a lot of interest in where we live from across the world due to the exotic northern lights. The sometimes-dancing aurora borealis occur at high earth latitudes when supercharged electrons from the solar wind interact with elements in the earth's atmosphere. These moving curtains of colors can be green, blue, red, purple, pink, white, or variations of rainbow colors. Japanese tourists fly to Yellowknife to try to see the aurora borealis. The Japanese tourists are brave. They board buses in the early-morning darkness and drive around looking at the lights, trying to find a good photo-shooting spot for them. The aurora borealis are as tricky as the ravens. They tend to only come out on crisp, clear, freezing-cold nights with temperatures like -40°C. So northerners tend to peek out their front door, go, "Oh, look at those magnificent northern lights," and run back into the house to watch them from behind their windows.

Alert

Some northerners have been posted to the most remote places like Alert, Nunavut, located 850 miles from the North Pole. Military and scientific personnel have been up there on rotation. One former weatherman spent an entire winter there in an Atco trailer with nothing around but snow. On average, there are about ten months of snow coverage at Alert. The July temperature can be in the 3.4°C range. The record low wind chill for the year was -64.7°C. I believe the weatherman didn't venture outside much unless necessary — to check the weather.

Interest in the North and Local Celebrities

The local celebrities visiting Yellowknife have been the result of a few television shows that were generated here, largely due to the interest of others in the uniqueness of being in the North and dealing with cold-weather hardships. TV shows that have highlighted the Yellowknife area have included *Ice Road Truckers* and *Buffalo Joe's Ice Pilots*.

The great thing is that the marketing surrounding these shows has really helped to put Yellowknife, Northwest Territories, on the map. This has really improved things for when northerners go south and are asked, "Where do you live?"

"Yellowknife."

"Is that in the Yukon?"

"No, actually it's in the Northwest Territories."

Before these reality-TV hits, you would see a blank-look curtain cross people's faces and hear the gear boxes in their brains turn—"I think that's in Australia somewhere, Northwest Territories..." Then they would go silent as they really didn't know where you were from and didn't want to make a faux pas trying to guess.

What to Drive in Winter

Nearly thirty years ago, most of the four-wheelers that made it up the rough-and-tumble highway to Yellowknife were pickup trucks. There were almost no sports cars in town. Due to bumps and grooves in the unpaved roads, lowriders wouldn't have made it and would probably drop a muffler along the way. Since that time, the government completed paving the highway from the south into town, and now there are all kinds of lowrider sports cars around.

Surviving Power Outages

One afternoon the power went out everywhere for two hours. Nothing in town had lights on, and everything was closed. As there were no computers, no TV, and no working ovens, we went for a drive. The cause this time was a mechanical problem, and the backup system didn't kick in. Sometimes the ravens knock out the power when they are burnt on a wire. I told my son, "It will come back on for 'Coronation Street,'" and sure enough it was back before my favorite show started. My next favorite television show is watching the Saskatchewan Roughriders play CFL football.

The worst power outage occurred when we were cooking a turkey in Inuvik. The power was out for many hours. We had to toss the turkey as the bacteria had started to devour the stuffing.

This morning the power was off again. There went a nice restful sleep. An alarm beeped all night, and, ignoring it, we went back to sleep. It was mild here at 2°C, so I was not too worried about the pipes freezing. At about 7:30 a.m., Hubby got up, started the generator, and put the furnace on, so it was toasty again. He looked up the emergency number for the power company to complain and told me their number has three sixes in it. So we now call it the Hell Number. They got the power back on while we were out for breakfast.

Car Extension Cords

People driving away from their houses with their car batteries still plugged in is a longstanding joke around here. One can view vehicles struggling up hills, trailing twenty-foot outdoor extension cords like dog tails until the ends catch under a tire and rip the cords right out of the cars. When driving anywhere in winter, one can see these shredded cords along the roads. Occasionally, someone will stop and scoop up one that's not ruined to replace his or her own shredded cord. Some visitors from California do not understand why we plug in our cars with extension cords; they think we all have electric cars in northern Canada.

Flat Tires in Winter

Everyone has had his or her share of flat tires in winter. Tire pressure dips in direct proportion to the temperature gauge. Most drivers get flats at night when no garages are open. Flats also tend to happen when the driver is at the farthest point from home, such as on the Dempster Highway near Inuvik in a ferocious blizzard.

One time we were driving through rain on the Dempster Highway near Dawson, heading for Eagle Plains, when we heard the *thump, thump, thump*—flat tire. We couldn't loosen the lug nuts as they had been put on by a giddy mechanic with a super-deluxe air ratchet.

The rain turned to snow, and then the snow turned into a blizzard. The temperature hovered just below zero. It was the second week of September, or what people down south call *fall*. For us, winter. We had to unload the van to lighten it to change the flat. We set our groceries on the ground, and they slithered down the mud-and-snow-encrusted embankment. There was also a fake six-foot-high wooden birdcage that my friend had bought to decorate her new apartment. The flat tire got replaced, and then we reloaded the groceries and birdcage.

It was six hours to the next gas station, and we persisted on our way. A continuous pulse of snow darted toward our eyes, in effect, hypnotizing us. Then we started hallucinating. My friend saw fictitious people waiting at a nonexistent bus stop alongside the road. I saw a ghost of a man in a prison uniform hunched over beside a rock.

The snow fell so heavily that my friend had to get out and walk beside the van to tell me where the road ended. A kaleidoscope of snow swirled toward us as we tried to keep the van away from the embankment.

I recalled my Arctic-survival-training course. My instructor had gone into the Nahanni Park area in June and got stuck in a blizzard wearing shorts. He spent the night in a lean-to then walked out into three-foot drifts the next morning. He was lucky to survive. He taught us to expect the unexpected. This trip certainly lived up to that expectation. The van crawled into Eagle Plains doing five miles an hour.

Hairy Leg News

Let's just say we got to the motel at 5:00 a.m., put the car into park, turned the ignition off, and fell asleep in our seats from exhaustion. Zombielike, we woke up every twenty minutes, turned the air vents on, and then switched them off again to preserve the fuel. By this time, the in-van heater had died, and we just had cold air circulating. After we woke up in whiteout stupors, we checked into the motel at about 7:00 a.m.

The next day the roads weren't much better when we started up a steep hill. We hit the crest and saw him barreling toward us—Fred the big rig driver coming full speed up the hill. Due to the winter road conditions, we were both driving in the center of the road. You couldn't tell where the road ended and the ditch began. Our eyes got really big, and I knew I'd have to get out of the way. I braked, slammed the van into reverse, backed up, and tucked the van as far over as I could to the side of the road. Fred shot past us in his truck like an F-18. The van leaned to the left and then to the right as the airburst pulled us from side to side. I looked at my friend and remarked, "Let's not do that again anytime soon." We both laughed out of relief.

With ashen complexions and shocks of sudden white hair, we continued driving. It got weirder. After leaving Eagle Plains, our first sighting on the road was not a grader as we had hoped. It was two guys coming toward us on World War

II motorbikes, wearing leather headgear like Baron Manfred Von Richthofen. Only this time we were not hallucinating. We had Paul Shaffer music playing loud. It was a song where the musicians were at "The World's Most Dangerous Party," and Paul Shaffer was talking to Eartha Kitt. Somehow hearing a party in New York seemed comforting in this desolate place.

By the time we reached our destination, I was sure I had strep throat and ran up to the emergency ward. Behind curtain number one was a fellow who explained that he was there because a horse had stomped on his foot during the local parade. Behind curtain number two another guy explained that he just put one butt cheek down on his car seat, and his back went out. I explained that I probably had strep throat as the heater in my van died during a twelve-hour road trip. I'm sure the emergency ward hears it all.

Snow Brush Approach

Someone in the south tried to perform a robbery using a car snow brush under his winter jacket. Whoa, that's truly Canadian. "Wow, buddy what are you planning to do with that snow brush? Take it easy and put that snow brush down, and no one will get hurt." One wonders how many getaway cars had to be pushed out of snowbanks with dead batteries. It certainly puts a damper on cold-weather robberies.

Moving in Winter

"The average person moves eleven times in his or her life-time," just came echoing over the kitchen radio. I have moved twenty-three times in my life. OK, so double the average. During my son's first year out of college, he moved three times in one year. Thankfully he had only a desk, a bed, his mechanic's tools, and two cars to move. Moving the contents of an entire house is like an episode of *Hoarders*. Why do people keep paper bags and empty boxes or string and old boots? They hold on to old outboard motors that haven't seen a launch date since the dirty '30s.

Moving in a Canadian winter takes guts or a taste for life on the edge. We moved into our Yellowknife home in December. There is nothing like having open doors when it is -30°C outside. You can see your foggy breath inside the house. Once the stiff, frozen boxes were thawed, we could start unpacking.

Signs of People Moving in Winter

It is January, and our neighbors have put their red canoe onto their SUV. This is the first sign that they are executing a winter move to the south. They have the barbecue, lounge chair, and sleds all lined up along the front fence, ready to go. Next someone shows up to deconstruct the shed. Yes, these are clues of an impending move in January.

Moving Van Slogan

There is a small moving trailer parked curbside in four feet of snow with a slogan that essentially says, "Move yourself and save money." The irony is that the neighbor's minivan pulling the moving trailer pooped out from the cold after it crawled twenty meters from where it was parked. Moving costs just went up due to the now-required van repairs, and the owner hasn't "moved" anywhere except out of his parking spot.

Gravel Truck

Another winter image is the city's gravel truck steaming by like a heavily armored dreadnought. This is how Yellowknifers deal with slippery streets. The exhaust leaves a cloud of haze for a block. The truck belches gravel out the back end like a bad case of bird diarrhea.

The purpose of the gravel is so that cars don't slide through intersections or roadways on black ice. In Ontario they use salt, which corrodes and rusts cars to the point where there are big holes in the bodies. The circulating cartoon about Ontario rust is a snapshot of drivers putting their luggage into the trunk and the bags falling through, smacking their feet.

Hallucination or Reality?

On the hallucinating front, the other day I saw a young man in a fall coat and gloves riding a unicycle. Actually it was reality because this fellow really does exist. He rides his unicycle in all seasons, including winter, around Yellowknife. This young lad is much braver than I am. If I pedaled a unicycle on icy sidewalks, I would end up in a face plant in the first snowbank.

Wild Animals of the North

Opening the front door in winter makes me apprehensive. There could be a wild fox sitting right on my front doorstep. When placing the garbage out back in spring, I also look over my shoulder for bears coming out of hibernation.

Some of the wild animals I've seen up close and personal around the north include a raven chasing a muskrat and huge, swimming beavers. I have seen foxes with red, silver or white fur. Eagles, ravens, and seagulls fly over our house near Yellowknife Bay at Great Slave Lake. I've seen porcupine, bison on the highway, black bears, moose, and deer.

While traveling in the Inuvik region of the Northwest Territories, I've also seen a reindeer herd near Tuktoyaktuk, muskox in Sachs Harbour, and caribou near Fort McPherson.

Some of the wild animals I've seen actually have personalities. The foxes run routes up and down our streets and cul-de-sacs that lead them onto the rock outcrops behind our houses. They scavenge whatever food they can find. The foxes look both ways before crossing the street, which always makes me grin. This tells me that they have adjusted to living in the city.

The groups of muskox around Ikaahuk, formerly Sachs Harbour, are very quiet, docile animals if not disturbed. If the herd is threatened, the adults face outward in a stationary circle, to protect their calves. When you stare into the eyes of a muskox or bison, it is like looking into the eyes of something that has been on this earth for millions of years. They have that ancient-knowledge look about them. When we see bison on the highway between Yellowknife and Fort Providence, we slow down, turn down the car radio, and stop. Once they move over to the side of the road, we speed up quickly to get past them. For the most part they are harmless, but during mating season it can be sketchy, and a bull might charge the vehicle. Personally, I don't view a Chevy Impala as competition for a mate in the bison family, but I guess they don't differentiate between animal and loud, fast machine, and they just view the vehicle as a threat.

One time the bison, like a youth gang in hoodies, took over a small community. They circled the village and were hanging out at the playground. People couldn't move their vehicles because the bison were everywhere. It almost brought the community to a standstill.

Ravens

The ravens are scouts, scavengers, and messengers of the North, hopping down the streets in search of overturned garbage cans. Sometimes they work in groups to nudge the lids off, rock the cans, and pick in pecking order from the buffet line.

The ravens are the tricksters, and they know how to get food. If you're sitting in a car, eating takeout burgers, they land on your hood and watch in the hope that you will toss them a French fry. I didn't know birds ate French fries, but apparently they eat them as well as cheeseburgers. They also drink the frozen pop by pecking at the paper cup. They are known to frequent chicken joints and are adept at holding paper cups in their beaks and pulling the lids off condiment containers to eat barbecue sauce and ketchup.

Our friend Fred once had two steaks ready for the barbecue. Fred put one piece of meat on the grill and went into the house to get some hot, spicy sauce. When he returned, all that was left was the package with the cello wrap flapping in the breeze. A raven had swooped in for a gourmet steak dinner with no surcharge. Lesson number one: always cover your steaks with something like titanium while barbecuing in the North and do not leave them on an open grill unattended.

Another lesson is to not leave groceries in the back of a pickup truck while you return inside the store for the rest of your grocery bags. Ravens can spot a roast in the back of a pickup truck and peck holes in it like woodpeckers while the roast's owner is back in the store.

As a test to confirm how smart the ravens are, a local placed powdered white donuts outside in the white snow to observe if the ravens could see the donuts from where they perched and distinguish them as food. All we know is that the donuts disappeared.

As messengers, the ravens work in groups and pass their messages down the street, which is especially noticeable on garbage can pick-up day. They have so many different calls—a lot more than just a caw. I would describe it as variations of trills, coo-coos, cloink-cloinks, and the warning squawks of high alert. I believe they have a repertoire of hundreds of different calls. They will position a scout raven on a light standard, and the rest will perch strategically on rooftops all along the block on garbage day. The scout tells them that it's OK to proceed. At this point, they start removing garbage can lids by knocking over the cans. Or sometimes a dog will assist them with knocking over the cans, and then it is feeding time. My husband said he once saw a raven lift an empty six-pack of beer still in the plastic rings right out of the garbage can.

I once saw a raven who thought that he was the hood ornament on a van. He hopped on the roof of this white van, spread his wings, and rode the van for at least a block. I almost choked on my cigarette. I give the ravens a lot of credit for their intelligence, and I believe you can never underestimate a raven. Hitchin' a ride—how smart is that? Van surfing!

Ptarmigan

In Yellowknife there are willow ptarmigan, and in winter they have a nice, white, fluffy coat of feathers. They look like giant snowballs with two tiny black beads for eyes. These birds are known for their small brains, which are reportedly smaller than their eyes.

When ptarmigan see a car speeding down the road, they obliviously walk toward the front of it. Locals jokingly call them "bumper fodder" or "northern chickens." They often end up as fox food. One time my husband was out hunting ptarmigan. He drew his rifle at a flock of them sitting quietly in a tree. *Blanff!* One bird dropped to the ground. All the other ptarmigans in the tree just stayed put, staring at the bird that fell and thinking, *What the heck happened to Fred?* Not one of them flew away. They had no sense of fear. That doesn't equate to a long life for ptarmigan.

They also make absurd laughing chuckles like you would hear in a house of mirrors at an amusement park. I am certain that if they saw themselves in the mirror, they would be frightened. But they still would not waddle or fly away. They really have no clue.

Moose

My sole encounter with moose was during rutting season. A bull moose chased a female moose, aka *cow*, up onto the highway right beside our van. They missed the van by about six inches and then veered off into the bushes. I had to pull over to let my startled reflexes settle back to normal. Incidentally, moose are way bigger than they appear in photographs or side-view mirrors.

Top Reasons Yellowknife Is a Great Place to Be in Wintertime

- No lines at the beach and lots of parking available once they plow the road.
- Your winter clothing wardrobe gets the most usage nine months of the year.
- Your twenty-year-old summer clothing always looks newly purchased.
- You never have to worry about a heat wave.

Hairy Leg News

- You can take a snow machine out as a regular vehicle.
- If you are a homebody, winter is your time to shine.
- Sunglasses are for whiteouts and blizzards.
- Blizzards wipe the snow off your car for you.
- There are no crocodiles in the Arctic.
- Availability of shopping carts is stellar because the wheels are frozen onto the parking lots.

Two

Northern Seasons

Spring in the North

It is mid-May, and I'm wearing sandals, no socks, a hoodie, and long black slacks. The temperature is "plus one" or 1°C. We now have daylight until 10:00 p.m. The roadways look like dust generators on a movie set. Welcome to spring in the North. After surviving nine months of winter and knowing we have a twelve-week summer, we scrunch our hastily painted toes into our dust-encased sandals.

Spring Decorating

Northerners like to stretch out their Christmas decorations through to the spring. They leave up all their outdoor lights, ornaments, and wreaths until April or May. This tactic is to get through the dark, depressing, long winter months until the snow finally melts. So in spring, driving down the roads of suburbia, I can see all those decorations and Christmas wreaths on door fronts pretty much until May, when we finally start getting puddles in Yellowknife. Usually the decorations are taken down about the same time that we start planting seeds in our gardens. Also around this time the city of Yellowknife's crews are busy thawing culverts, pumping puddles, and doing regular road maintenance. With the spring snowmelt, drainage water can accumulate in basements, under trailers, or in backyards. Our solution is to dig drainage channels through the hardpack snow, similar to the Netherlands' dikes on a miniature scale.

Spring in northern communities brings other odd sightings. For Muskrat Jamboree in Inuvik, there is a photo on Facebook of a pickup truck pulling a framed tent down the ice road. Another typical sight in Yellowknife is the fellow sliding by on a bike, wearing sunglasses and a backpack and gripping a hockey stick across the handlebars.

It is the end of March, and the street is still a mix of snow, ice, and pavement. A for-sale sign on a house in our neighborhood has been hidden under five inches of sticky snow for most of the winter. The property agent must be wondering why the house is not selling. Once during the five winter months, we saw footprints in the snow going up to the sign, and the snow had been wiped off; it was covered again within days. Today the snow has melted off in a cascading sheet as we hit a beautiful 7°C.

Hairy-Leg Contest

Since it is the end of March, Yellowknife holds a Long John Jamboree celebration on the plowed ice of Yellowknife Bay. There is an ice castle, ice-sculpting contest, hairy-leg contest, bonfire, and fireworks. I expect there will be a lot of contestants in the hairy-leg contest. A lot of women go all winter without shaving their legs because they wear pants for the cold weather. As a joke, some actually put tiny rubber bands around the long hair standing out on their legs— like little hairy-leg ponytails or braids in winter. Eventually, women may choose to shave their legs after months of letting the hair grow to keep their legs warmer.

One spring in late April we went to our local patio distributor and trotted home with some Adirondack plastic chairs whose red, yellow, and green colors replicated the Mexican flag. We assembled the patio table in -3°C with frozen fingers, a few screws and caps a-flying.

Once we were finished, we got out a bottle of bubbly, invited the neighbor to join us, and christened the table. Fred was telling us about how high winds took his umbrella table airborne, and when it landed, the glass top shattered into a pile of rubble. My husband mumbled something like, "Yeah, tempered glass."

We wore winter jackets, and I had a blanket wrapped around me like a sushi roll while we commiserated over the thirty-kilometer winds. The scene reminded me of shivering on metal end-zone seats at CFL football games, trying to warm our hands around the coffee thermos. Bring on the coffee!

Spring Street Cleaning

The Yellowknife city crews place street sand or crushed quarry gravel on city roads during the winter to reduce slippery driving. In the spring, the snow melts to reveal streets covered in sand and dust that get cleaned up by the street sweepers. According to the city's official newsletter, there are 164.9 kilometers of paved streets and alleys in Yellowknife. Who knew?

Silly Season

The aftermath of winter's cabin fever is what northerners dub the "silly season." We see it all the time at work, where the change of season coincides with the March fiscal year-end. People's tempers are short. An edgy whine creeps into their voices. Northerners pretty much just go, "Oh, it's silly season." People are always blowing up over the last cracker around this time of year. It's just the season for letting off steam.

Summer

There are many things to do in the North during our three months of summer, which start in June. In Yellowknife's great outdoors, there is incredible fishing on the Big Lake, as we call it, boating, and golfing. I myself like the indoor sport of watching football on television.

Hare Today, Goon Tomorrow

One time, a giant hare ran across the field in the middle of the CFL football game. Man, he was fast. The camera operator switched the focus from the game and followed the hare twice around the field, and then the bunny went flying out of the gate. It was way more interesting than what was happening on the field. Seriously.

Football Starting Time

My favorite football team's game didn't start until 3:00 p.m. That meant I had time to kill, so I did all this puttering around the house. Tuning in just before three, I found that there were just two minutes left in the game! Argh! I had for-gotten that the ads for the games post the Eastern time, not Mountain Standard time. So I watched the last two minutes. Grrrrrrrrrrrr. Then I got up and made some of those chicken rollups, where you pound them with a hammer, layer on the Swiss cheese and ham, and then roll them up and grrrrill them in butter. That was good cooking therapy.

Go, Riders!

It is well-known among my friends and family that my fa-vorite CFL football team since the 1970s has been the Saskatchewan Roughriders. Go, Green! They have been my team of choice ever since watching football with my dad and brother. My dad was from Saskatchewan. It just happens that being a big fan entails having the right gear displaying the Saskatchewan Roughriders logo. This includes an oven mitt, mug, flag, decal, ball caps, golf caps, computer mouse, lawn gnome bank, and miniature gnome. Team supporters can go to www.riderville.com or www.theriderstore.ca for more information. I am still saving up to get the Riders' BBQ cover if it is still available.

Seasons of Small-Town Life

One summer, our street started looking like an old Western movie. I could visualize the tumbleweed cartwheeling down the road. There was no one outside except for one young woman pushing a baby carriage with a tiny dog on a leash, the meter-reader pinball deflecting into driveways, and a raven mimicking a vulture swirling overhead. A skinny squirrel leapt across the road like a prairie gopher.

The blur of dust revealed a sole pickup truck bouncing by, and that was it for activity or humanity in our neighborhood. Yes, Yellowknife was looking like an old Western movie, a one-horse town. Each fall, we would take the dead plants unceremoniously off the deck and proceed to shovel. Yes, that's snow in the fall, folks.

We watched the vent-cleaning truck, with billowing pillows puffing up from the truck like the Pillsbury doughboy on helium. Once every two weeks, the garbage truck attendants made an appearance, and there were the occasional Real-Estate guys and the fuel-truck deliveries.

The ravens scoped out the garbage cans on garbage day. If they saw food, they gathered as much as they could in their beaks and flew off, and then another raven showed up to finish off the picnic. It's funny seeing a raven with an entire bagel in its beak. Other than that, not much was going on during the weekdays on our street. In spring, snowmen were leaning backward doing the limbo as they slowly melted into the ground. Some snowmen skewered themselves onto a small tree beside them.

Winter and Not Winter

By mid-September we can get snow in Yellowknife, so we start putting away our plants as soon as we see minus temperatures. All the lawn accessories are stored away, garden hoses disconnected, and taps turned off. Gardening implements are hidden in the shed. Most depressing is when we bring the shovels up to the front of the house again in anticipation of another year of winter.

Our spring and fall in Yellowknife are like two weeks. We go from parka to spring jacket for two weeks, and then it is T-shirt weather. In fact, a lot of our conversations and humor come from the weather. We joke that there are really only two seasons in the North—winter and not winter.

Three

HOMEMAKING IN THE GREAT WHITE NORTH

Women in the North have several choices: go to work, stay at home, or a blend of both. Either way, they are still trying to find things to do in the wintertime. Here are some great time wasters.

Northern Garage Sales

Garage sales in the North can be tricky. One year I went to a garage sale on May 13 and slipped on black ice. I ended up in the hospital with a broken leg. The joke at work was, "Don't send her shopping."

One weekend our family decided to have a garage sale. We had items such as throwback furniture, the kind when the telephone table existed before the days when phones were capable of hanging off walls and numbers were stored somewhere in the rotary memoirs of telephone operators.

Items not for sale included our CD music ensemble. Suitcases are a big seller and make annual appearances at our garage sales.

Favorite Soap-Opera Apparel

My favorite British soap opera was in "minor character week" again. Even the major plotline was losing its shine. One ratings booster was the barmaid's barely there outfit. The actress had the body of a dancer. In comparison, I have the body of a German folk-dancing hausfrau with hairy winter legs minus the lederhosen.

What to Wear in Winter

When I first came to northern Canada nearly three decades ago, January and February were a frozen solid -40°C. Many people came here for six months to see if they liked it. They walked to work in a five-star parka and ski pants. They walked like Frankenstein in the huge stovepipe boots of the 1980s— "moon boots"—the closest thing to which today would be Sorel's Intrepid Explorer boots. The only exposed flesh was the tip of the nose. Some decades later, we now have milder temperatures in January, and they can be as high as -10°C. Global warming has had an impact.

Rethinking Northern Uniforms

The poor guy working at the local drive-thru window the other day was wearing a short-sleeved uniform in -40°C. The head office needs to rethink their uniforms for northern climates. He was handing bags of food to customers with his bare hands. How about long-sleeved turtlenecks with downy vests, toques with a logo, and gloves?

Tips for Staying Warm in Winter

A magazine article laid out the tips for how to stay warm in winter. It was the usual: dress in layers, make sure you're well fed, and remember the extremities. My tips for staying warm in winter are move to a warmer climate or stay inside and drink lots of coffee.

Braids and Hair, Hair, Hair

After a much-anticipated January escape to the Caribbean, I came back with mini-braids in my hair. It took two women working for an hour to put them in. When it came time to take them out, the braids were all matted, knotted, and a mess. It took three grown people to get the knots out, resulting in poofy hair. There were photos of my knots on someone's Facebook page. Recommendation: take the braids out a lot sooner.

Lazy Susan Just Got Lazier

The top shelf of our lazy Susan collapsed under the weight of four cans in our rotating pantry. Our home is the handyman special. Seriously.

Refrigerator on Wheels

In the wintertime, you don't have to worry about leftovers from restaurants going bad in a warm car. It becomes a refrigerator or freezer on wheels. It is much the same for groceries. We transport food in our vehicles in frigid temperatures, and food can be left in the cars overnight when the temperatures are in the minuses. It's a great place to store a turkey for Christmas. If individuals need a smoke break, they can warm up themselves and their cars, with the cars becoming sofas on wheels.

Dishwasher-Loading Zigzag Trick

Often when I'm doing housework, my imagination kicks in to avoid the drudgery. For instance, when I'm loading plastic knives into the dishwasher basket, I envision that I am a magician sticking knives into a box where my assistant is enclosed, and then the assistant pops out unscathed. The magician's box has been designed so that the blades put into it are deflected at the handle, or the assistant has been lowered through the stage floor and reappears after the knives have been removed. Voila. Dishes done.

Accidental Floor-Cleaning Tip

A bar of glycerin soap accidentally dropped into our dishwasher after it overturned in a container and wasn't noticed. As a result, we had about two inches of bubbles and water on our kitchen floor, and our floor has never been more sparkly! The bar of soap is really clean, and the kitchen floor glimmered for months.

Kitchen Booby Traps

When I was opening the kitchen cabinets above the stove, the sesame oil got caught on the door rack that holds the spices and went flying onto the nice clean kitchen floor and onto my dress. Now the kitchen and I smelled like Chinese food. Note to self: sesame oil needs to go further back on the shelf or onto another shelf.

Other booby traps encountered in our kitchen are as follows:

- Upon my opening the freezer door, giant frozen blocks of chicken stock stored in plastic bags torpedoed out of the freezer onto my foot.
- Exploding two-liter bottles of pop rolled out of the fridge like bowling balls.
- Knives flew out of the knife drawer like it was a surprised porcupine.

Hausfrau Injuries

At our house, it is safety first. However, some minor hausfrau injuries have happened during housework. One time I was doing the laundry and stepped onto a rubber carpet that turned out to be floating on drainage water; my feet flew out from under me, and my back smacked hard against the laundry sink, making for a painful kidney for a few days. From then on I donned an orange safety vest and helmet and announced to the family, "I'm going in there now!"

When I was taking a pie from the lower rack of the oven, my wrists hit the upper rack and started sizzling.

Another mishap was sliding down the carpeted stairs on sock feet. Fortunately I landed on my derriere.

Tripping over extension cords still plugged into cars and careening over boots in the front entrance are other hausfrau hazards.

Then there is smacking one's middle or baby toe on chair legs.

Vertigo

One morning I woke up at exactly 4:44 a.m. That day I had vertigo, a rash over my eye, a sty in my eye, and my inside ankle tendon gave me grief. The vertigo was brought on by doing a half gainer on a black-iced parking lot the day before.

Wacko.

Ready with a warm tea bag to draw out the poison from the sty, I put the bag on my eye. The mirror reflected what looked like a drunken pirate. Still dizzy, I flopped back into bed with a tea-bag patch over my eye and went back to sleep. Arrrrhhh!

Typical January Weekend

This one day neither of our neighbor Sally's vehicles started. We boosted both of her vehicles' batteries. Then her other neighbor needed a boost, so we boosted her car as well. In between boosting, we all sat at Sally's place drinking eggnog. It took all afternoon to boost the cars in the neighborhood. The eggnog made it take longer.

Hairy Leg News

Our friend Ken just had a transmission drop out of the truck he just won in a raffle. Lovely. Maybe it's a factory recall?

After the vehicle roundups, I went home and made spaghetti sauce, and it was on to a Disney flick. I tried to check e-mail. The Inuvik server was down, and the Ottawa, Ontario, and Aylmer, Quebec, servers were down due to a couple of days of severe ice rain. Power lines were down, ergo the Internet too. I heard rumblings of soup being made upstairs, so I might have had some time to read for a bit. I decided to have a leisurely bath.

We got the kids some bowling shirts that needed a wash. There is that word again—laundry. We have a leaking washing machine. Note to hubby: "No, I'm not in a rush for the leaking machine to be fixed. It's only been a few weeks now, and I like walking around with sopping-wet socks. It makes me feel like a queen living on a yacht." The next day I watched sports on TV. Did I mention that I had strep throat from the day before?

Winter Decorating

Living in an icy climate is great for generating decorating ideas. One novel way to decorate is take a canoe, let it fill with snow, and plunk down three cut evergreens into it. Ice candles are another way to go. They make great monuments of igloos, ice castles, pyramids, or art deco on the front lawn.

Bay Leaves

While making spaghetti sauce, I discovered that we had run out of bay leaves. I called the neighbors' house, and their teenage son answered the phone.

"Hi, Tyrone, do you have any bay leaves?"

"Just a moment, I'll check." Long pause. "No, we only have vodka."

"Oh, I'm making spaghetti sauce. Not Bailey's, *bay leaves*."

"Oh."

"Hold that thought. There might be a need for the vodka for the cook."

A Man's Idea of Cooking

Our friend Fred warmed up some premade grocery-store Chinese food, which he says he "cooked" by adding ingredients from a mixed vegetable freezer bag.

Hairy Leg News

This may be slightly sexist, but here goes…

How a woman reheats a single, previously cooked pork chop:

- Place pork chop on small plate.
- Insert pork chop into microwave oven.
- Hit 1½ minutes.
- Serve on small plate.

How a man cooks a single, already cooked pork chop:

- Get out the *largest skillet* in the house that resembles a wok.
- Get out the *largest cutting board and largest knife* known to man.
- Take up the *entire counter* to dice a few pieces of green bean.
- Add rice already precooked by wifey-poo.
- Dice the single pork chop into six chunks.
- Insert the ingredients into the wok.
- Flip the ingredients with the *biggest wooden spoon* one can find, resembling one used to stir a witch's cauldron.
- Put results on the *biggest plate* in the kitchen.
- Find the *biggest glass* in the house and fill with water.

- Eat the results of this gastronomic bouquet that's the best in the land according to said male.
- Burp and declare it the "*best* meal ever."

Enough said.

Men's Cooking Tips

I picked up some men's magazines at the grocery store and decided to see how they handle cooking tips. Well, it's not called "cooking"; it's called "assembling." A loose quote is, "Form burger meat into the shape of an indented hockey puck. Assemble garnishes on top. Cook in a hot iron skillet."

A woman's magazine would state, "Make burger patties, add ingredients, and cook to taste in a frying pan." Apparently, men don't cook; they assemble. Also they don't use "kitchen knives"; they use "chef's knives." And they don't make "hamburgers"; instead they make gourmet rubber hockey pucks. They are master gurus of the kitchen. Women are viewed as hausfraus.

Two Thumbs Up with Veggies

My son was reminding me of the time when both he and his older brother came home at lunchtime from elementary school. On the same day, the older son had a door slammed on his thumb, and, due to boredom, the youngest was picking at dried chewing gum when he got his thumb stuck under a chair. The result: they both had frozen bags of peas on their hands and kept each other company for the afternoon while watching television.

Vegetable Stickers

I don't know what twisted person decided to put stickers on green peppers, but I've found them chopped up in home-made spaghetti sauces, quiches, and casseroles. For some reason, I almost always forget, dice the pepper, and think of it afterward. Would you like some stickers with that spaghetti sauce?

Pumpkin Puree

March 14 is "pi" day (3.14 on the calendar). I had been making pumpkin pies for years, and sometimes they would turn out OK, and sometimes not at all until...discovery! My husband pulled the "pumpkin-pie filling" can out of the garbage and announced, "Oh, that's not pie filling; it is pumpkin puree." You're kidding me, right? Who knew? So the result was this gawdawful pumpkin pie that I had made without a recipe. I'd just winged it and forgot to add the brown sugar. It was bland and horrible. That explains why all these years some of my pies turned out delicious and some did not. There are two kinds of pumpkin in cans! It was suggested that next time I might try using a recipe book.

Laundry-Mode Surprise

It's been so long since the towels were washed that they have morphed into anthropoids and walked themselves to the washing machine.

I'd just moved the laundry from the washer to the dryer when I spotted something at the bottom of the machine. *What is that?* I wondered. As my younger brother would jokingly say, "It's a sup-prise." It was the remote control for the TV set. It must have gotten mixed up in the bed sheets. It's nice and shiny now. I don't want to zap myself turning on the TV, so I will wait awhile before I try the remote control. And the bonus is that the numbers are still intact.

Power Outages and Cinnamon Buns

A decision was made to bake homemade cinnamon buns, which might calm my son's flulike stomach, the cinnamon especially. So I finally got those done. The brown sugar was rock hard, so I nuked it for a minute, and that seemed to do it. Funny, I never see tips for "rock-hard brown-sugar fixes" other than the old stick-a-slice-of-bread-in-the-sugar-bag trick. Microwaving it works to a point. When I put the buns into the oven, however, the power went out. They turned out not bad after an extra hour of rising time. We've had so many power outages, my son said it is starting to feel like we don't pay our power bills, but we do.

Vacuum That Sucks

I accidentally sucked up some "fake snow cotton batting" from the Christmas decorations, and it hooped my vacuum cleaner. My husband performed scalpel surgery on the vacuum hose and duct taped it. It sucks to be me.

Fire Alarm

A fire truck and ambulance rolled up to my neighbor Sally's place, and she came out in her pajamas with her arms flapping in the air to talk to the firefighters. It seems she burnt the toast, which set off the fire alarm, and she has a house alarm system, which automatically dialed the fire crew. The firefighters were joking, "Sorry, but we have to take a picture of the 'evidence.'" They then proceeded to snap photos of the burnt toast. We will be teasing her about that for a long time to come. My husband asked if we should bring over marshmallows.

Burning the Debit Card

My friend had her debit card in an envelope, and it got tossed with a bunch of empty envelopes into her wood stove. I've heard of cold, hard cash but never hot-flash cash in a wood-stove. I heard the bank employees had a good laugh at her explanation for needing a replacement card.

In menopause, our memories aren't what they used to be, and we get so distracted that we do odd things such as trying to put a house key into the car's ignition or putting the aspirin in the fridge and the dirty glass back on the shelf.

Shoparama

Lately I've had the habit of adding the extender "arama" to everything. Cramming a year's worth of clothes shopping into one weekend I call "shoparama." Winning five hundred dollars on a one-dollar Keno ticket, "flukearama." Dancing for five hours once a year, "dancearama." It works for just about everything. I am hooked on adding "arama" to everything. Is this what they call my obsession? I am now writing a "bookarama" after going for a drive, "spinarama."

Novel-Writing Course

I was just snickering to myself as I took a "novel-writing course" two weeks ago, and I haven't even had time to type up the notes from the course. How would I then have time to write a novel? There must be a course called "How to make time to write a novel" or timearama.

Not Awake

I came up with these gems first thing this morning in my 7:00 a.m. waking-up haze.

You know you're not awake when you:

a) Put your house key in your car ignition and wonder why the key won't fit.
b) Brush your teeth with antiseptic cream.
c) Take a vitamin, put the glass back in the cupboard, and put the vitamin bottle in the dishwasher.
d) Drive past your destination and then circle the block wondering how you did that.
e) Try to light your cigarette with the car radio volume control.
f) Put the garbage out on the wrong day.
g) Put the coffee pot on but forget to put in the coffee grounds.
h) Reach into the fridge for a beer.
i) Put on two unmatched socks, put your pants on inside out, and forget to brush your hair; as well, the dryer fabric-softener sheet is dangling out the bottom of your pant leg.

Nancy Gardiner

j) Forget your computer's password, so you try whimsical ones such as the following:

- Gizmo lives here
- Kilgore was here
- You want it when?
- Survey, what survey?
- Guacamole—is that the correct spelling?
- Honk if you love Jesus!
- Ferd Berfle lives here
- Cancun can't be that far from here—really
- Spideyman was here
- The Tasmanian Devil is my vacuum cleaner
- Message on the sewage scooper truck: And you think your job sucks!
- Have you seen my car's extension cord?
- Fifty bucks gets you a high-end coffee
- Gas or ***, no one rides for free
- Meet me in Nantucket
- Far from the madding crowd
- Surely, Shirley, Sandy Doorman can't know it all?
- Where's my hat?
- About that Maserati benefits package
- Meet me in St. Louis or Fort Good Hope
- Who moved my cheese and cummerbund?
- Freedom is just another word for nothing left to lose or wealthy independence

- Peace, brother!
- Hip-hop, hibby to the hibby, hip-hop, don't stop rockin'!
- The mothership has landed in our backyard
- Two tickets to reality please
- Circus? Was there a circus in town?
- Killer Klowns from Outer Space meet Godzilla
- Not broken, just bent P!nk
- Bombastic Bushkin
- Abracadabra, hocus-pocus, dominocus
- Arrivederci, Roma
- Pass the ashtray
- Pass the tequila, Sheila
- Keith Richards is cool!
- Alice Cooper is also cool!
- Darlene Love is super cool!
- Chocolate, bacon or poutine?
- Would you like fries with that?

Matching Paint Chips to *Coronation Street*

I was undecided about paint colors, and it occurred to me to hold the paint chip up to the wall of Eileen's home on the British TV show *Coronation Street*. She has a neat mauve. It was tough as they kept switching scenes, but I held the chip to Eileen's wall, and I think this will be our color for an accent wall. Perfect. Inspiration can come from anywhere, even a soap opera.

Glamor Grunge Is In

Glamor grunge, which they are calling *glunge* or *big* hair, is in. This means big hair like in the '80s, such as the B-52s had; so the beehive is back. Aaargh, no hair spray! They have a special curling iron that makes the hair poofy. Glunge it is, or just wear a ponytail. I personally prefer wash-and-go hair. I also have my awesome hairstylist on speed dial.

Taxes Going Up

The start of a new year hails the government's solution to the deficit—raise taxes. There are many ways Canadians deal with this. They can put their credit cards into the deep freezer, hiding them under a frozen turkey. Or they can find more creative ways of dealing with a financial pinch, such as cutting back on frills or selling junk. I am not good at doing any of those things.

Women's Magazines

A lot of women's magazines are full of tips for beauty regimes and organizing. Sometimes the material seems to be recycled from one magazine to another. In other words, some freelancers are making a killing recycling "tips" and "how-to" content, such as how to stay athletic, how to look seven years younger, and how to have baby-soft skin using avocado and olive oil. There are also the weight-loss tips such as how to lose three pounds of belly fat. Also rampant are tips on how to "declutter" or "how to organize" and "how to make the most use of available space in the home."

It's all pretty much the same for every woman's magazine I have read: formula, formula, formula, and very repetitive. I have a theory that you could buy just one woman's magazine, and that would be it for a lifetime as all the others are relatively the same.

The subliminal message in these magazines is "women should do this, women should do that" and that we're not up to snuff unless we do all that stuff.

It would be great to pick up a woman's magazine with headlines that bellow the following:

- Order out; forget home cooking.
- Be content with what you own.
- You're perfect the way you are; don't change a thing.
- Don't waste your money on the overpriced clothes featured in this magazine; try flea markets.

- You don't need to be a gourmet cook and perfect mother to have it all.
- It's OK to be a stay-at-home mom, formerly known as "housewife," if that is what you choose.
- Some models in this magazine have had plastic surgery, are airbrushed, and their arms look like celery sticks. Please don't try to live up to these standards.
- Microwaving—unlocking the key to family meals.
- Dial-a-Pizza—every home should do this on Fridays.
- Tips for families to know where their stuff is without asking their mother.
- Tips for families to pick up after themselves.
- Tips for families to do their own laundry and dishes and to help with house cleaning.
- Tips for families on how to treat moms with gift certificates for massages and not pots or pans for Mother's Day.
- Tips for families to acknowledge the work their moms do for them.
- True-life story: we threw out the iron and ironing board when our son jumped off the top bunk bed and turned the ironing board into a V-shape of twisted metal.
- Tips for buying clothes that are only wash-and-wear and don't involve ironing.
- Tips to steam clothes near a shower.

- Forget making a big turkey and ham for Christmas and spending all day in the kitchen. That was for women who stayed home all day, every day. Take your family to a nice hotel for a meal or order in KFC. Tip: you can preorder a bucket of chicken and freeze it and then thaw when ready, or read up on the joys of TV dinners and *The Joy of Not Cooking, Just Reheating*.
- How to arrange thumb tacks on your cork board in the shape of a clown fish to relieve boredom.
- How to clean up after a boiled egg has exploded in the microwave.

Tips for Women Living in Cold Climates

There are many handy tips to help women survive in cold climates.

How to:

- Fix the snow blower when your husband is out of town. Tip: buy a new one.
- Avoid having a cardiac while shoveling two feet of heavy snow. Tip: befriend Kevin, the guy with the loader.
- Scrape your windshield. Tip: use a credit card.

Nancy Gardiner

- Recognize the signs of a storm coming and when to cover your Maserati before the first snowflake. Tip: when it is cold and the wind is howling, you know these are early warning signs that it'll be winter faster than you can say "abracadabra," "Copacabana," or "lederhosen." Look to the clouds.
- Close your van door when it's stuck open in forty below zero. Tip: pull over to a garage and ask someone nicely to help you.
- Get the most from your car heater when the car is designed for living in Arizona. Tip: have two car heaters installed.
- Have summer tires in winter—not an option. Tip: get the treads that look like the wallpaper pattern for a Sherman tank.
- Install chains on your tires for climbing mountains in wintertime. Tip: find a good garage.
- Hook up the red and black jumper cables to a dead battery without zapping yourself. Tip: research the Internet for proper procedures or ask someone in the know.
- Take sunny vacations. Tip: start planning them at least a year in advance and earn enough money to pay for vacation dreams implanted in our brains by the women's magazines telling us we can afford to travel regularly.

Hairy Leg News

- Dream of retirement in a tropical climate. Tip: research sunny retirement havens that don't involve hurricanes, tornados, or water deprivation.
- Think license plates that involve palm trees. Tip: find license plates that do not display the words "brrrrr" or "shiver."

Four

Subarctic Living

There are many tactics for surviving suburbia in northern climates. One is to find nice winter vacation spots on beaches or historic sites to see at tourist destinations. Other strategies are making your own fun and being creative. Here are some examples of how northerners get through winters in suburbia.

Barbecue Pranks

I was thinking up funny pranks, and a few sprang to mind. My prank idea focused on the neighbor's barbecue. This couple, well, they are both super cooks, and whatever is on their barbecue always looks great. I was drooling over their beautiful pork roast and thought about switching in a tiny burnt one as a joke. I never actually did it but thought it would be hilarious!

A guy at work wanted to grow something, so we got him some carrot seeds. He planted one, and the next day we brought in a full-grown baby carrot and inserted it into the plant soil. When he got to work, he acted surprised.

The Facebook Phenomena

It sat there in my e-mail for a year. "Dave suggested you like WORLD ROCK SYMPHONY ORCHESTRA." OK, I was curious about the all caps, but aside from that I was not really one for Facebook. I check mine twice a year, and I tell people that so that I won't raise their expectations. So far it's working. My favorite Facebook post was from Fred, who was "checking out tomatoes" at the Byward Market in Ottawa, Ontario.

Sewer Slogans

The fellows who drive around in the trucks that suck out the sewage from houses in Yellowknife that are not connected to the sewer system have a great sense of humor. The sign on the back of their trucks reads, "And you think your job sucks." These trucks are not to be confused with the water-delivery trucks, which have the slogan "Nectar of the gods."

Speaking Italiano and Isolated Post

My husband gave me two CDs on how to speak Italian. I launch them into the car while driving down the highway. I am not actually going anywhere as it takes about fifteen hours to get to a real city from here, so normally I just take a spin with my drive-thru coffee, turn around, and come back. It's kind of like that old black-and-white TV series *The Prisoner*. The guy keeps trying to escape but always ends up coming back. That is what it is like living in an isolated post. At least we have a road out of Yellowknife. Some isolated posts are fly-in only.

Sonnez le Ding-Dong

Ring the ding-dong—or *sonnez le ding-dong* in French—is our annual golfing chant. When we get halfway through the course, we ring a bell at the midway point. Sometimes I also jokingly use this expression for people who ask the obvious.

Advertising

I have a bucketful of ads in my e-mail. Things like *Haute cash free* and *Exclusive bargain coupons* and *Ten dollars off every pair of stretchy jeans you buy*.

My reaction: I don't know what *haute cash* is, but I bet it is not free; *exclusive* coupons for a store in some country where I never shop are useless; and I never wear jeans.

Hello, Coo Coo is one of my favorite spams.

Dog's Bowl of Water with a Twist

My neighbor Sally came over for a brief visit on the deck with her teenage son Ken and Rickie the dog. We had a bit of a gabfest. They drank water with lemon on the side, and the dog had a bowl of water. Rickie is getting old—he's eleven years old and was looking for shade, and there was none on the deck. He didn't want to drink or eat anything. We were observing that the poor dog wasn't drinking the bowl of water because it didn't have lemon in it.

Rather Large Dog

A teeny, weeny car drove by with this Marmaduke-type humongous dog in the back seat. The dog was bigger than the car, and his head was scrunched down. The dog took up the entire backseat sideways. The car did not match the dog. Were they going to the veterinarian? Marmaduke was not amused.

Quantum Physics and Willie Nelson

The TV show *Nova* did a cool episode about quantum physics. They presented it in a way that was interesting and not like high-school science classes. They showed Bohr's and

Einstein's theories, which clashed. Einstein said there was a parallel universe to ours, there was "certainty" in how things would turn out, and life was predetermined. Bohr said it was "random and uncertain." One tends to trust Einstein on this one. It was never resolved, and the scientists are still coming up with equations. The cool part is that they think teleportation like in *Star Trek* is possible but a long way off. No more waiting in airport lines.

Of course, I'm sure they'll find a way for people to pay for this service in the future. And, oh, the parallel universe is the exact opposite of this universe. So if we teleported ourselves to it, it would probably be all perfect. Remind me to teleport myself to the other universe. Or maybe I'll just teleport Willie Nelson music to the other universe, no offense to Willie.

Mother Nature

An adolescent male goose has fallen in love with a few plastic ducks and a goose decoy strategically placed on the water of the local bay. The real goose brings the decoy food, nurtures it, and cuddles up to it at night. The live goose blends in so well, some people think he's a decoy too. We're not sure if he flies south that he won't try to take the decoy with him. No rational explanation has been offered for the goose's behavior toward the decoy goose. Is July–August mating season for geese?

Tweeting

They were saying on the news that some politician was tweeting, "I'm eating a banana now." I don't get Twitter but found that particular line pretty funny. Seriously, does anybody care about this stuff? I have dubbed it Tweetarama, Tweetfest, and Psychedelic Sweet Tweets.

Excerpts from My Facebook Entries

- Eating apple squares with berries.
- Picked some Saskatoon berries today. Wow, the excitement never ends.

Painting *Interrupted*

My husband came home a day earlier than expected from his fishing trip due to high winds. Of course, I was in the middle of my deep mauve paint job on the living room and dining room accent walls. Eek, Batman—painting *interrupted*! I'd also bought a hutch, which was sitting upside down so we could put a middle support beam under it. All the stuff from the china cabinet was in bins in a spare room. To sum it up, the place was a disaster. Fortunately, the last coat was just drying when my husband walked in the front door. My Spidey sense was right; my husband hates changes. But he is adjusting to the new paint job and hutch.

Waiting for Doctors

A doctor who is not my regular doctor entered the examining room as I was cleaning out my purse and organizing my bills. The doctor apologized for taking so long. I had seriously thought of filling out my income tax forms while waiting for him to appear.

One time the doctor's staff actually forgot me in the waiting room with the door closed. At 5:40 p.m. they opened the door as they were turning out the lights and informed me that the doctor had left for the day. They had forgotten that I was there. What a self-esteem-boosting moment.

Who Says Women Don't Exercise Enough?

Here is a summary of household exercises performed regularly—daily or weekly—and repeated ad nauseam:

- **Weightlifting**: lifting bags of school supplies, groceries, and laundry; making box store runs for potting soil; moving furniture around the house with minimal help from the males in the family; straining to lift the overfilled garbage cans with broken wheels to the curb.
- **Stretching:** washing floors, walls, and ceilings; painting; mowing the lawn; trying to cut toenails.

Hairy Leg News

- **Bending:** reaching into the freezer, washing machine, and dryer.
- **Arm lifts:** washing and blow-drying hair, putting things back on shelves that household members never put back.
- **Arm circles:** stirring spaghetti sauce and toilet bowl cleaning but not at the same time.
- **Endurance training:** running on four hours of sleep on a daily basis without complaining.
- **Fear factor:** crawling around on rooftops, measuring replacement roof tiles, while harboring a secret fear of heights.
- **Use of fine motor skills and tinier muscles:** cooking every day, grating cheese manually, lifting pots, washing and scrubbing pots that won't fit into the dishwasher. Incidentally, recommendation: don't buy anything unless it goes in a dishwasher.
- **Upper shelving or walls clean and jerk:** placing objets d'art, such as Cellini's gold-plated salt shaker, onto higher shelves or hanging artworks of curiosity, such as my son's elementary-school 3-D papier-mâché model of a dragster.
- **Shuffling boxes for larger muscle groups:** shuffling around other household members' boxes in the basement, attic, closets, garage, or sheds until they can claim them many years later after college or university, moving apartments, and finally settling

down into a permanent residence. Incidentally, they won't want the stuff by then as it's so outdated, but think of the exercise you've had over the years re-shuffling all those boxes.

- **Sweeping movements:** sweeping floors, vacuuming, washing the car interior/exterior, picking up items that household members drop and don't pick up, dusting cobwebs off the ceilings with a broom, straddling the broom and going for a ride down the street.

- **Stairmaster**: lugging laundry up and down the stairs or crawling up high ladders to put up Christmas lights or to paint the ceiling.

Preferred Exercises

Here are some preferred exercises for women:

- **Digit dexterity:** dialing Molly Maid, caterers, pizza joints, and local restaurants.

- **Elbow bending:** drinking beer de rigueur at a local pub, similar to a *Li'l Abner* cartoon.

- **Jumping jacks:** going to concerts for musicians who you want to hear sing and play music to see them in person and not on TV or the Internet; showing fan appreciation with jumping jacks at concerts.

- **Scouting**: searching for good locations on a beach to place a towel.

Hairy Leg News

- **Shoparama:** finding good stores along the beach that are more than T-shirt or beach-towel kiosks.
- **Squats**: picking up seashells, laying beach towel down, and picking it up when done.
- **Pretzel maneuvers**: playing Twister on the beach and beach volleyball.
- **One-hand catch:** playing Frisbee on the beach.
- **Neck twists left to right:** trying to cross a busy street right beside the beach.
- **Dancehall movements:** attending the local dancehall located right on the beach and dancing to disco music until 3:00 a.m. and sleeping in the next day.
- **Slotarama:** Using one-armed bandits to develop biceps.
- **Adult quiet time:** Seeking out peace, silence, and serenity or uninterrupted blocks of "me" time. No matter how old the other family members are, most women crave this and are adult-quiet-time deprived.

Code of Conduct for Family Members for Adult Quiet Time

Women should have the ability to do the following:

- Sleep in without being woken up abruptly by phones, alarm clocks, or deliveries for other household members.

- Make plans without family members trying to change them.
- Read a book uninterrupted from cover to cover.
- Watch a TV show without someone trying to change the channel.
- Listen to music without someone trying to change the channel.
- Stay in the bathroom with the door closed without someone knocking on the door or trying to slip a note under the door asking, "What are you doing in there, and how long will this take?"
- Have a clear thought without losing it in midstream when a household member asks where something is that he or she is responsible for putting away.
- Have a private telephone conversation with a girlfriend or other relative without interruptions of nonstop chattering or "Come see this!" or "Where's my...?"

Winter Coffee Angst

Once I was outside in my rubber fishing boots, pink fuzzy bathrobe, and fake fur coat, with my coffee cup sitting on the railing, and the cup stuck to the railing. I pulled with all my might, finally got the cup off the railing, and half the coffee erupted. So I'm out there at 2:00 a.m., laughing out loud, and no one's around. Of course, I could always watch *The Shopping Channel* for even more amusement.

Hairy Leg News

Northern Donuts

It is well-known in the Arctic that anyone stopping in Yellowknife will likely bring dozens of donuts back to their small, remote communities. You can see passengers at the airport with clear bags holding boxes of two dozen or more donuts as carry-on luggage. Once back home, some would bring them to sports groups, family functions, or meetings. One meeting I was at included the deluxe donut packs. The chocolate glazed were the first to go, followed by apple cinnamon and honey glazed. If people get to the boxes late, all that is left are the white-powdered donuts that dribble dots down your suit. Looking like victims of a baby-powder attack, people are left with white rings around their mouths like mimes. Then the jam-packed innards come oozing out in one big blob. They try to put the entire donut into their mouths. Their cheeks bulge, and they can't chew. This was when my boss asked me, "So, how are you enjoying Inuvik?" I nodded with my bulging cheeks: "Mmm...yes," and excused myself with a wave of my hand.

Fast-Food Outlet

Stopped at a fast-food joint for a quick grilled cheese for me and a cheeseburger "that tasted like a mustard and ketchup sandwich" for my husband. He never eats fast food. He must have been really hungry because he ate the whole thing.

Concert Ride Sponsor Is a Funeral Home

Interesting tidbit, a funeral home sponsored drives home from a recent concert. My first thought: does that mean they give us rides home in the hearse? Apparently, they just sponsor the rides home on a shuttle bus. Phew.

Palm-Tree Decal Installation on Front Door

I decided to try putting a decorative palm-tree sticker on my front door right after breakfast. The sticker came with "easy" nine-point instructions: Make sure the window is wet...do not apply on shiny side. It was impossible to tell which side was the shiny, and it only became obvious after two attempts when it wouldn't stick. Then it stuck, but it wasn't centered, and I had to reapply. By the time my husband got home for lunch, it was up.

Food-Is-Ready Chimes

One time the local greasy spoon installed a new dinger for when the cook's food was ready for pickup by the server. It was to the tune of "Off we go into the wild blue yonder... da, da, da" done in organ chimes. It was a scream, and I noticed they silenced it after a few weeks, probably with a big fat pot lid.

Best-Ever Shortbread-Cookie Recipe

This is the best shortbread-cookie recipe I have ever found, and it belongs in a book, so here it is:

1 cup butter
1½ cups flour
1 cup powdered sugar
1 tablespoon vanilla

- Chill dough, knead dough lots.
  Actually if you chill the dough for three hours in the fridge, you will need to nuke the dough ball for forty seconds as it comes out of the fridge like a bowling ball.
- Roll out to one-quarter- or one-half-inch thick.
- Cut and top with a center dab of honey to hold the candied cherries onto the cookie…yummy!
- Enjoy!

Bake at 350°F on middle rack for fifteen to twenty minutes. Cool, serve, and enjoy!

Five

WORKING NORTH OF 60°

No matter how cold it gets outside, we still have to go to work. Many jobs are outdoors up North, even though it can be -40°C or colder. Northerners have found ways of coping with this, most of which boil down to dressing for the weather. Here are some northern work stories.

Work-to-Sleep Ratio (WSR)

The work-to-sleep ratio (WSR) for me lately has been 80:20. I am starting to look like a bag lady at work, a situation impacted by the males of my household monopolizing the shower and bathroom every morning. Adding to the challenge of the ever-occupied bathroom is the odd 3:00 a.m. snowplow beeper.

While most women look polished at work, I look like I dropped the Amy Vanderbilt clothing etiquette book like a football in the mud and adopted Sasquatch as my role model. An extreme makeover would be a nice start.

Anxiety

There is a TV show on tonight about anxiety—work- and home-induced anxiety. People are stressed out. Employers are always trying to "do more with less," which means less help, fewer staff members, less money, fewer jobs, and less peace of mind.

On top of work overload, people now download all the services they used to purchase in person. So the "self-serve" age has become too much. People pump their own gas, they are their own bank tellers at ATMs, and they bag their own groceries. All the niceties of life are just about gone. No wonder people have anxiety. The pace of life is too fast. The last home-delivery milkman in the world retired a while ago. What a sad end to a chapter of someone coming to your house who wasn't trying to sell a magazine subscription.

Lost Lunch Hour

A friend of ours named Fred started his day with a teleconference booked over the lunch hour. As he left his apartment building, he was met with a sign in the parking lot: "Remove all vehicles right away for snow removal, no excuses and no exceptions." Of course, Fred's vehicle would not start and had a soft tire. He dashed to the landlord's office. The landlord, Mr. Buster, was prepared for anything. He flew to the filing cabinet, drew long and hard on his old stogie, and pulled out a copy of Fred's lease agreement. The florescent light made his bald head appear to give off its own light source. "Yes, indeed, all cars in the lot must be operational. Says so right here in this lease agreement. Tow it, or it will be removed at your expense."

When Mr. Buster was back outside in the parking lot, he wore a toque two sizes too small, adorned with a pompom. A gruff beard framed his puffy, diamond-shaped jowls. Mr. Buster watched as Fred tried a tire sealant. It did half the job but wouldn't do, so he grabbed the tire and hailed a cab. Hopping in with tire in hand, Fred had the tire fixed and returned to find another flat tire. Someone helped him with jumper cables to start his engine. With a pushing-coasting maneuver, Fred careened his car back into the snow-filled spot. He went back to check under the car hood. *Swack*. Silence. His mind took a moment to interpret the data. All of the car doors were locked, and the car keys were still in the ignition. Fred could not believe it. He ran back to his car with a metal hanger to try to break in. Now he was really running late for work and running out of gas.

By this time his cheeks were burning from the cold, and his forehead was hot.

After less than an hour, he pushed on his car window and was able to get into his car. Fred turned off the car and raced back to work late. He had missed the teleconference. Fred thought to himself that maybe it is better not to know in advance how your day is going to go.

Work Teleconferences

I hate taking teleconference calls over the lunch hour when it involves another region of the country and that's their "best time to do it." Imagine if Marco Polo had to call into our teleconference: "Hi, there. Nothing big to report, but I did find some new spices for that two-day *tourtière* recipe you want to try out." Genghis Khan: "My elephants are lined up as an attack wall at the border. Is this phone call going to take long?" Columbus: "I thought it was North America, but I guess I was wrong. The coffee is good here. Send more coffee filters, and could you pick up some creamers?"

Northern Teleconference

The northern teleconference can go something like this. Everyone gathers around the black UFO box on the table.

Someone on the Nunavut end of the crackling, sizzling telephone explains that the lines are bad and they can barely hear us. The earth stops as we adjust the cords. We all start shouting into the UFO box. For the next three hours, we continue to shout our comments. If we were shy before, we aren't anymore.

Reasons for Losing Cell Phones

Some of the best reasons I've heard for losing a cell phone include dropping it into a paint bucket and losing it overboard from a shirt pocket while bringing a fish into the boat. Explaining those lost cell phone scenarios is always priceless. Statistics say the top places for losing cell phones are coffee shops and bars. It must be caused by the distraction of everyone diving into the Timbits box or ordering more beer. Cell phones work all right in winter, but it is helpful to tuck them into inside parka pockets if people are dependent upon them.

Motivational Posters

Ever notice that so-called motivational posters are really putdowns of other people? Such as "Originality" with a bunch of people taking photos of themselves pretending to hold up the Leaning Tower of Pisa.

I would like to see a motivational poster: "How to get through the day without blowing a gasket."

Work Memo: Keeping Ferdie in the Loop
Memo you didn't receive previously

Dear staff member or other politically correct salutation:

My workplace alter ego, Ferdie Berfel, is special and will not be confused by any mixed messages, subliminal messages, or any other kinds of messages. She will be kept in the loop at all times and will be notified when Santa leaves the North Pole to deliver presents. She will also be notified of any potlucks, brunches, and food-snack days so that she can add to her expanding waistline from being stuck inside all winter. She will be contacted for any required offsite field trips and will be the first in line to get that work trip to Las Vegas for research.

She will have the first metered parking spot at the front door so that she can carry her soda pop home with the least amount of aggravation. In addition, when choosing decorations for her office, she will get first pick of the good ones.

Please forward all food memos to Ferdie so that she can add to her fabulous figure.

Signed,
Keeping Ferdie in the Loop!

Winter Work Escapes—Safety Training in Las Vegas

There was a course offered on safety tips for professionals. Hmm, workplace safety in Vegas? Uh, don't stick your hand up the slot machine to try to loosen change. Don't shake the one-dollar machine too spryly or it may land on your foot. Don't ride in a convertible down the Vegas strip with your hands up in the air waving your cowboy hat—keep your hands in the car. Don't walk the strip with multitudes of souvenir bags dangling off your wrists. And your bad shoes can cause blisters. Also, don't take the gondola ride without a life preserver.

Computer Moments

Have you ever pressed a computer key and the whole e-mail that you were writing was obliterated? I used to retype the whole thing. Then I remembered that all I have to do is press the back arrow on the top menu bar, and it all comes back. It would have been great to think of that before blanking many e-mails and becoming what is known as a "retypist."

Business Call

While I was working on my computer in my home office, my son was playing on his computer. I was on the telephone making a business call, and all you could hear was this loud burping in the ambience of my home. My son was playing a computer game where this animal burps every two seconds. We will turn down the volume for the next phone call.

Carpal Tunnel Princess

I had a short-term contract as a typist and spent many hours on the computer. Sally nicknamed me the "carpal tunnel princess." My fondness for typing quickly collapsed after that contract. My other friend Kylie got a similar job, and we called her the "cataract queen." She started developing dry eyes from the computer time. She also abandoned ship on that job and decided to be a stay-at-home mom for a few years.

Kylie and I used to work at the same job, and we were always invited for the special-occasion buffets just in time for the last squishy tomato and wilted piece of lettuce. We used to laugh about the timing of our invitations.

Putrid Start to a Day

Often, I can tell the way a day is going to go from the get-go. It's like the old Yiddish saying my father used to tell me about: "The way it starts is the way it ends." It is one of those days where someone innocently walks into work expecting a happy day. There's tarp, plumbing pipes on the floor, and a bad smell. The ceiling tiles have been pried off, leaving drywall bits below. A stench hits the nose with the full force of a jet blast. *Phew*. The emergency plumbing crew pried the pipes apart, revealing coffee grounds and food stuff congealed in the flat part of the pipes. Even the plumber's snake can't handle the job. The pipes are so compacted with grime that the putrid smell of mummified food fills the hallway for most of the day.

The plumber was disgusted by the foul odor even though he encounters a lot in his line of work. In addition, the array of disgustingness laid out on a tarp on the floor included a shop vacuum, pipes, and buckets of murky, wretch-inducing gray-beige water.

What a charming way to start the day! This didn't meet my fantasy of Rod Stewart and a kilt-clad hairy-legged

Scottish pipe band serenading me on a red carpet as I stepped off the elevator. No luck either on that imaginary round of golf at St. Andrews golf course in Scotland after work.

Photocopier

One of my prior work experiences included something about static and carpeting in the photocopy room that no one else seemed to notice. There were also the accordion paper jams that took at least two coworkers to figure out using every letter of the alphabet; the letters identified the machine parts. After opening every fissure of the machine for days, we finally decided to call the repairman. Go figure. We performed basic surgery on our photocopy machine, which always leaves a tiny piece of crumpled paper in its bowels. Managed to fix the machine parts a, b, c, d, e, and f. No swear words were used this week. Remember the days when you only had to open the door to clear the photocopier, and it would work again? Now you have to be an astrophysicist and alphabetologist to get the machine working again.

Why is it that when I finally got to the photocopier, I was caught dealing with the aftermath of the photocopy repairman's visit? All the paper reams in the machine were static-like, and a leftover screwdriver was discovered under the display glass as I tried to crunch out some humongous urgent report. The report incidentally needed to be in page order and not on accordion paper. We have decided that our copier should be set ablaze like a Viking funeral pyre and shoved over a waterfall.

Time-Management Tips

There are some handy online management tips, and one of them was to only read your e-mails in the mornings and not in the afternoons. Sounds more like "how to get yourself fired" tips to me.

Ides of March Vacation-Day Request

I have always been superstitious, and Shakespeare's "beware the ides of March" has always made me nervous around March 15 to the point where I take the day off if possible. Wasn't it the day when Brutus stabbed Caesar in the back?

Of course things happen all throughout the year, but they seem more pronounced on this day for some reason. I am only aware of one casualty so far this year, and that's a friend who got a concussion from snowmobiling and is in recovery mode. But that could happen any time. I still walk around corners more carefully on that particular day.

Calling into Work Late, Sick, or Dead

The most creative excuses that I have heard for not coming in to work include "bad pizza," someone who thought he or she had won the lottery, and someone whose cat had puked. Bad excuses for quitting work include someone who was in need of a makeover, someone who wanted to learn how to play the trombone, and someone whose dog had the chickenpox.

Southerners Who Come North for Jobs

People from the south will often try the North for jobs. They may come up for six months or two years to "try it out." Some stay three decades. Some others don't stay long. One time a fellow came up to Inuvik for a job. He stood at the top of the airplane's staircase after his plane landed, turned his head 180 degrees, declared, "Uh, no," and got back on the same plane he had come up on and left the North. He had not even set foot on the ground. Others have tried to stay longer. People from down south either leave in a hurry or embrace the North. A lot of it has to do with lifestyle. If they enjoy snowmobiling, boating, camping, dog sledding, and outdoor activities, this can be a good fit for them. Movie watching is another great pastime. When we lived in Inuvik, I believe I'd seen all the comedy movies ever put on a reel-to-reel.

Civil-Servant Bus Ride

It was raining in sheets when we saw people walking home and getting soaked after work. Almost no one uses an umbrella in Yellowknife. It rarely rains hard, as we are considered a virtual desert. But on this day it poured rain like I had never seen except once in Ottawa thirty years ago. The Ottawa incident involved about a hundred civil servants lined up at the bus stop after a tough day at work. A bus driver, sensing the hilarity of it all, drove past everyone, tires veering into the expansive water puddle, sending a wall of water over everyone waiting for the bus. A collective shriek went into the air. People holding umbrellas were all soaked as the icy water erupted from ankle level upward.

The bus driver kept going, his jet-propelled bus slicing through traffic like a juggernaut on butter. This is clearly called "bus driver angst." I could envision his backward head tilt and hear his evil laughter—"Bwah-ha-ha"—as he raced to the next stop six blocks down, too far for any of us to catch up and give him our anticipated dry-cleaning bills or shake our umbrellas at him and give him a piece of our minds. That mental image will always be with me no matter where I live.

High Winds and Civil-Servant Snowstorms

Another seven inches of snow fell right around the time that public servants go home. I had a bird's-eye view outside my work window of the KFC bucket when I worked for the Government of the Northwest Territories. One day I glanced out my window to the scene down below. The usual civil-servant snowstorm starts at around 5:00 p.m. with ninety-kilometer winds. After work someone sailed across the street on black ice and grabbed a car door handle on the other side of the road. It was howling. My windows at work were shaking, and the flags outside looked like the wardrobe of someone marooned on a desert island.

Meanwhile, at the airport, two incoming planes couldn't land and turned back. One northern pilot who has bricks in his pants landed anyway.

Job Calls

I was joking with my son that if anyone called for me about a job, he couldn't let on that I was off to Mexico—no singing or humming Mexican music and no ocean-wave noises in the background.

"Just tell them that your mom plans on checking her e-mails. Be mysterious."

One time, when I was a substitute teacher, one of the young students asked what I did when I disappeared to work in the evenings after school. I told him I was working on Hansard—transcribing verbatim reports and proceedings of the NWT Legislative Assembly on a Dictaphone machine. The student took *Hansard* to mean *hamster* and assumed that for the previous six weeks I'd been "working on getting a pet hamster."

Fox and Angel Food Cake

One day on my way to work, a fox was happily prancing down a back laneway with an entire angel food cake, still in its package, dangling from his jaws. Startled when I came around the corner, he dropped it, and then, realizing this human wasn't about to steal his food, picked it up in his mouth again and pranced away a little faster. Obviously he was feeding his family. I have a lot of respect for that.

Appears Not to Be Working

It seems as though you can work five hours straight, and the moment you stop to look out your window is the exact moment someone walks into your office, and it appears you are not working. It's also the moment you might perchance be examining your fingernails for length or filing them.

Campfire Suggestions for New Employee Courses

Over the campfire this summer we had lots of good laughs about all the courses companies could offer their employees. The ideas included Agenda Writing 1, 2, 3, and 4, Fire Making 101 and 102, How to Hold a Meeting, How to Speed Up a Meeting, How to Shut Down a Meeting, and How to Shut Down Excessive Talkers Who Take Over Meetings.

The Ideal Job

Here are some perks that I believe would make employees feel they have the ideal job:

- Spa days.
- For lunches, red-checkered spaghetti bibs are permitted.
- Free paid gym passes as the ideal employer values health and wellness.
- No Internet blocks so that employees can do their banking at work, check out the weather for the weekend, and peruse their stock market picks with regularity.
- Free coffee, muffins, and lunches brought to the worksite by a gastronomic genius contractor.
- New policy: wear whatever you want to wear. Low cleavage, spike heels de rigueur, cutoff jeans and hot pants, bandanas, funky nail colors, uber-bright-colored sequined clothes for meetings. Offbeat is supremo.

Tips for Women Reentering the Job Market

Reentering the job market can be scary. Here are some tips:

- Update skills via the Internet.
- Ask a friend or neighbor to help sort through your 1960s hippie clothes and decide what to donate.
- Read a woman's magazine on how to look ten years younger. I personally like the jumper Dorothy wore in Wizard of Oz as a fashion option. The red ruby shoes, a fashion statement. And, yes, pigtails can take years off one's face. Better yet, skip on the way to your interview with your picnic basket and bring a few friends along.
- Attend the interview with a smile on your face and a song in your heart: "Off to See the Wizard" is a good song. AC/DC's "Hell's Bells" is another good one.
- Read up on all the latest trends, electronic gadgets, and news. Know the industry you are applying for and the competition.
- When you are told in the interview about the job duties that you hate, use that poker face to mask the look of "Geez, you're kidding me, right?"
- If you are ignored by the receptionist when you walk in for the interview, this is a red flag. Chances are that he or she has applied for the same job that you want.

- If you got the interviewer's name wrong from the beginning, it might be better to leave right away.
- If the supervisor has the personality of a drill sergeant, run away!
- If your new office's desk is a rolling dessert cart, the computer is dead, and the office is a broom closet—run away!

Healthy Ways to Maintain the Absurdity at Work

- Do your nails with whiteout.
- Make chain-link jewelry using paper clips.
- Try whiting out an entire page, leaving one word intact.
- Mark off your days on the calendar with dinosaur stickers and gold stars.
- Write a cover letter in crayon.
- Line up a teleconference call and then change offices, leaving everyone scrambling, wondering who is calling where from where.
- When working for a radio station, leave your radio on for the entire day on the "other" station. Phone in to win prizes. Proudly display your new mug near your computer and wear the free T-shirt to work. Offer to share the free pizza with coworkers.

Nancy Gardiner

- Guffaw loudly at the news on the radio. Have the radio turned down low so no one else can hear it. When coworkers dash over to hear what's going on, quickly change the channel to fuzz.

- Ask coworkers to take your calls while booking your dream vacation.

- After accidentally dropping dots all over the floor from the three-hole punch, use scotch tape to pick them up.

- When filing, continually ask coworkers if "Mac" comes before "Mc."

- Rent a limo to bring you to and from work. Act mysterious.

- Don't bring in some small family photo in a five-by-seven-inch frame. No. Think big. Think video. Play videos of your family for coworkers.

- On greeting guests, make a drumroll announcement that so-and-so has arrived. Riverdance and cartwheel your way over to the coffee machine to offer coffee. Do a backflip over your chair. Do a cannonball into your chair and yell, "Tide's up." Spin the chair in a couple of donuts to the bookshelf. Punch the CD player onto Chumbawamba. Grab a book and pretend you are on a luge run as you roll back behind your desk. If it is Christmas, shake your jingle bells for a festive mood.

Hairy Leg News

- Don't diligently put the paper in the shredder one by one. Grab the entire document, staples and all, ram it in, and watch it smoke.
- Disclaimer: any resemblance of this fictional office to yours is purely coincidental.

Six

CHILDHOOD MEMORIES

While living in the North, it is quite common for the baby boomers to think back to how easy they had it when they were younger as opposed to having to haul their keisters into work every day in -40°C. Here are some reminiscences of the fabulous 1960s.

Toys of the 1960s

Thinking back to the 1960s, we can remember that the toys de rigueur back then were the Easy-Bake Oven and Barbie. If you didn't have either of those, you were a social outcast. No one could ever say my parents spoiled me. I had no Barbies and was told a few cake mixes in a regular oven amounted to the same thing. I did have a Tressy doll, where you pushed the belly button and her hair grew out of a hole in her head, which my parents tried to convince me was "better than Barbie." I didn't fall for it. We would go over to my cousins' place to play Barbie. They had super deluxe Barbies! Their Barbies had their own wardrobe carrying case, teeny plastic shoes, purses, ball gowns, swimsuits, homemade scarves, and a convertible car to get around town.

Growing up in Quebec

One time my mother asked me, an Anglophone elementary-school student in Quebec, to go to the grocery store to buy some grape soda pop. I walked a half a mile to the store and came back empty handed. "They didn't have any grape soda pop. All they had was 'raisin' pop—yech." She smiled, then explained that "raisin" is the French word for "grape." So it was back to the store to get some of that stuff. I turned a can around to see the word "grape"—who knew?

Childhood and Chalkboards

Watching an old movie triggered some childhood memories for me—chalk writing on a blackboard for one. Talkative children of the blackboard era recall being told to stay over lunch or after school to write one hundred times *I will not talk in class*. This was the first inkling that we had of our rebellious natures. My response was to take the chalk holder for drawing musical staffs, insert four pieces of chalk, and finish the job in one-fourth the time. Instead of writing *I will not talk in class* one hundred times, I wrote it twenty-five times. If my teacher ever noticed that my writing changed only once every four lines, she never said anything. I wonder if that is how efficiencies are discovered.

Pea Shooters

Kids in kindergarten in the early 1960s knew that pretty much everyone on the block wanted a peashooter. A peashooter consisted of a large straw and a bag of peas. Total cost to parent: two dollars. I was not allowed a peashooter as I "could put your eye out."

Firecrackers

Our other wish-list item was firecrackers. When we were visiting our cousins on an air-force base, we would get handfuls of them all attached together. We would lie on the side of a sand hill, light one fuse, and throw the whole string of them over the hill—*grack, pop, kapow!* Great fun until the military police stopped by and shut us down. My father let me know that kids were injuring themselves with them, so that was the end of firecrackers.

No Seatbelts

I recall rolling around under the backseat window of the car while it was moving, lying down in the back of a station wagon while on highways, and crawling on the floor of the car looking for a toy, also while in transit. The nodding doggy in the back window was more secure than I was. It seems to me that the 1957 Chevy did not come equipped with seatbelts or if it did, I was not aware of them.

One time when I was five years old my aunt gave me driving lessons. She had an old coral-hued Rambler, and the gears were push buttons on the dashboard. She would change them with her long nails peeking past the buttons, half-burnt cigarette between two fingers, and bracelets jangling. Sitting on her lap, I would turn the big steering wheel, which to me was like driving a bus because a steering wheel to a five-year-old is huge. We would drive down the main street while I shifted gears in my imagination. I should have received my driver's license way earlier than age sixteen.

Laneway

Growing up in Montreal across from Decarie Boulevard, we had laneways, which to kids were like travel arteries and instant playgrounds. The arteries would take us to kindergarten and our friends' places and were connected to all kinds of backyard mysteries.

One time, a group of us were walking down the laneway, and four-year-old Tommy went flying down the lane, screaming hysterically, arms flapping, crying. Not even the older kids with long legs could catch up to him. We finally overtook him a block later on the street near his home. When we were able to calm him down, we asked him what had happened. He had been walking barefoot down the laneway, stepped on a bumblebee, and it had stung him on the sole of his foot. To this day, we are all terrified of bees.

Handwriting 101

In elementary school, the letters of the alphabet in script and print hung above the chalkboard for us to look at and practice our handwriting skills. We would scribble continuous *O*s and *I*s in our scribblers, now referred to as lined notebooks. Penmanship was a big thing, and we took pride in our handwriting. It had to be legible.

We would sharpen our HB pencils at the group sharpener. This usually involved whirring, breaking off tips, more whirring, and the pencil sharpener jumping as it detached from its foothold, whirring onto the ground, and a laugh or two. The smell of pencil shavings nearly on fire from the friction singed the air. Some kids would grind their pencils down to nibs and take great glee in the challenge of writing with the smallest pencil stubs in their notebooks.

Hairy Leg News

The left-handers would have their notebooks angled at forty-five degrees on the desk with their hands wrapped around them in contorted positions, releasing their dread in *arghs* when they wrote in grade-four fountain pen. Their hands slid over the wet ink, smearing their writing into blotches—nothing an ink blotter could remedy.

Older kids told us they used to get their hands rapped with twelve-inch wooden rulers for writing with their left hands. There was an old wives' tale that was recounted in the playground that left-handedness was a sign of the devil. Seriously?

Skipping

At recess we would all run outside and—in warmer months—haul out the skipping ropes. For Double Dutch, two skipping ropes would be going at once, and timing them right took great hand-eye coordination. If the person controlling the ropes didn't like the kid skipping, he or she would raise it just a few inches off the ground so the kid would trip. Not cool.

Sewing Elastic

There were also long white half-inch thick sewing elastics, used for another playground pastime. Two kids would stand about six feet apart with the elastic wound around their ankles. The middle kid would then lift the elastic with his or her foot and hop around in the contorted elastic. It was kind of like cat in the cradle, with your feet and sewing elastic.

Jell-O

Most kids came to school with apples for recess. We would stand in the playground and eat our apples. The rare kid would turn up with a box of red Jell-O. Those kids would lick an index finger, dunk it into the Jell-O, and eat raw sugar. Their fingers and lips would be glowing bright candy red—the evidence. Oh, they would go back to class just wired and had a hard time sitting down for the rest of the day. In those days the Jell-O packets came with plastic wheels with likenesses of old-fashioned cars on them. At recess, we would trade and collect them.

Collecting

Growing up the 1960s, people could collect anything. Laundry soapboxes were resplendent with beach towels, cutlery, and all kinds of household items in them. One could set up a new home just from the prizes in the laundry soapboxes. One just had to be careful not to dump the prize into the washing machine with the soap.

Kids would also dig into the bottoms of cereal boxes to find prizes such as secret decoder rings or magnifying glasses, digging deep to locate the prize. Once the kids went to the bottom of the bag with their arms, scrounging around and displacing all the cereal so it was a single lump, this usually meant the bag would no longer fit back into the box it came in, much to the chagrin of the parents.

Back then, Cracker Jacks caramel popcorn—with the saluting sailor logo—had real mini toys in their boxes such as spinners, plastic figurines, or miniature puzzles. One brand of cigarettes, Rothmans in Quebec, gave coupons smokers could redeem for Corning Ware. One of the tea companies, Red Rose, gave little miniature figurines of animals and nursery-rhyme characters in their tea boxes. The porcelain figurines were made by Wade England.

Collecting grocery-store stamps was another pastime. If kids licked enough stamps onto a wad of papers that looked like bingo cards, their parents could hand in the completed book with some twelve hundred stamps in exchange for merchandise such as lounge furniture or water decanters. I recall at least one grocery chain had this customer-loyalty promotion.

In the 1960s, Canadian kids collected sports cards, trading cards, the plastic coins of automobiles and airplanes that came in boxes of Jell-O, and, of course, pennies. Another promotion featured a "surprise bag," which could be purchased for a nickel at the corner store. It contained cheap candy. By the early 1970s, the Esso Power NHL Player softcover album was rampant, and kids were collecting NHL player stickers to save in the albums. These were action shots of players in uniform and were fun to collect. This generation of kids is still collecting things to this day, such as old record albums.

Old Black-and-White Movies

An old black-and-white movie with Cary Grant, *His Girl Friday*, is on TV. I have seen it before. I love those old movies. They have two actors in them, one page of screen credits, and no distracting special effects. It's all about the story. Those were the days.

Charity Casino Fundraiser

One time when we lived in the south, my parents went to a "funny money" casino night that had been advertised to raise funds for charity. The event was raided by the police in full riot gear. My parents had believed it to be a legal charitable event. My dad, who was an off-duty policeman at the time, said he had never in his life seen people move so fast toward the exits. My guess is that my parents were allowed to leave after their identification was checked, or they hightailed it out of there before the police could find them. Maybe the organizers didn't have a permit?

Childhood

My childhood memories are a mishmash jammed together in no particular sequence.

I recall in kindergarten roaming the dump on an adventure and discovering a flat dead cat with no eyeballs. It was my first experience with death and totally freaked me out. It made me stop, pause, and look intensely at that cat. No eyeballs?

The schools back then seemed to have a strict code of conduct probably adopted from a gulag. In grade four I served a lunchtime detention for running down the stairs. I had been in a hurry to make it home for lunch. As punishment my teacher had me stand in a corner facing the wall the entire lunch hour. That was humiliating, and no lunch was served. Never ran down the stairs again.

For entertainment, we would put rubber balls in the toes of our mothers' nylon stockings, stand with our backs to a brick wall outside, and then whack the balls against the wall to a rhyme that started, "My mother told me…"

I remember stepping into a gigantic puddle that came to the top of my boots and wiping out on the ice underneath. It gave new meaning to the word *soaker* as I was cold and shivering, wet from forehead to toes. Nothing a good hot bath couldn't cure.

Once, our pet hamsters were frolicking on the back lawn when company arrived, and we forgot about them. When we finally remembered the hamsters about six hours later; they were long gone. As kids, we couldn't believe they weren't still there. No concept of time.

Old Movie Projectors

Before PowerPoint, there was the old 8mm home-movie projector. My dad would haul out his, and the noisy projector sounded like a jet engine starting up. This setup also required a screen and a tripod, which usually rolled up by accident or fell over in a heap.

Once we stopped laughing, the show began. There was no sound with the film, so we made our own comments as we went along—comments such as, "Oooh, look at that beehive hairdo!" or "How long did that pet salamander live?"

There were shots of thumbs, close ups of foreheads, and long shots of feet. Some earlier work included shots of blank skies. And there were lots of shots of the family walking toward the camera with cement smiles pasted on their faces like a cartoon. The best part about old silent films was that they left the viewer's imagination wide open. And you could watch the films in fast reverse as they rewound on the reel.

My Precious

There are memories of "my precious" growing up through the years. My first preciouses were bright colored marbles with cat's eyes, the giant ones being the Supremo Kings. Then one Christmas I received my first doll. I christened it Elizabeth, after the Queen. It had black curly hair and shocking blue eyes with giant eyelashes that moved with the eyelids. We would set her arm up to slowly wave at the crowds in a permanent royal wave.

One year later I received my first pair of metal roller skates. Kids would put their feet with shoes into the skates and tighten the key and then connect up the straps. The hex-like key was worn on a string around my neck, and that key was "my precious." If lost, no roller skating. Learning how to stop on roller skates was another one of those life lessons. Lesson #5,633: Do not grab on to other moving objects or tent poles to break a fall.

My next precious item was a new bike, which got stolen at the local shopping mall. While recounting my plight to a uniformed policeman at the mall, I had my first emotional implosion: burning tears amid choking, sobbing, sniveling, and not-quite-breathing sounds. The bike was later found at another shopping mall.

After the bike, I received my first pair of downhill skis. Following the skis, my first car, a 1969 convertible Cougar with a 351 Cleveland engine. *Varooooom!* After many lemony used cars, I finally graduated to a new Impala with all the bells and whistles.

Of course, the grand pooh-bah of "precious" was the birth of our children, along with all the beautiful memories my family has given me.

Approaching retirement, "my precious" has become the health of loved ones and myself, plus time spent with family and friends. I'd also include prolonged vacations spent doing what I want, when I want, and upgrades to my home front.

But the most precious thing is time, such as the precious odd day for me to do nothing.

Military Upbringing

Many of my friends and relatives had parents in the military, and I was the daughter of an RCMP member. My baby photograph was taken by the RCMP identification officer as a favor to my dad. How they got a baby to sit that still sideways for a profile shot on a woolen RCMP blanket still amazes me.

After talking with some of the military families I grew up with, I would like to share some examples of how we lived and some common traits that we noticed.

Generally, we do not call in to work late, sick, or dead. We were brought up to drag ourselves in to work, sick or not, no excuses, giving some of us a martyr complex about the common cold or flu.

We do walkabouts around the outside of our vehicles before we depart from the driveway. Similar to a pilot's checklist, this is done to check for inflated tires and cracks and leaks before starting the engine. Even now, we equip our vehicles with first-aid kits, blankets, flares, fireworks, candles, and enough food to feed a high-school football team.

Our pets are trained to heel. Our driveways are shoveled the moment the snowflakes hit the pavement. Our laundry is folded like it just came out of the plastic. Our garbage cans are placed outside the night before like Fred Flintstone. We do near salutes of appreciation to the garbage truck as it trundles down our street. We have learned how to fold tents neatly down to the size of a postage stamp. And we have been known to scrub around toilets with toothbrushes and clean hard to reach places on the stovetop with toothpicks.

We clean our kitchens like battleship galleys. We grew up with battleship linoleum on our floors, and we could communicate from enclosed places as if we were stationed on submarines—*ping, ping.* We can still eyeball a suspicious character in the neighborhood at two thousand meters and signal our neighbors with our blinds.

As we were growing up, there was very little that escaped our parents' notice, meaning we did not get away with a lot. We kept curfews, beds made, and laundry done.

Changing residences was a common occurrence for military and RCMP families when I was growing up. Because my father was always worried that he would be transferred, he was in his late forties when we finally bought our first house. For some children, this meant learning new schools on a continual basis. It meant being the "new kid," who no one talked to for at least a year. Most of our peers had been together since kindergarten. I remember going into grade seven, and I had one friend by Christmas. I tried to make sure I had at least one good, close friend and told myself that it was about "quality not quantity." We were always adapting to new environments, new rules, and new peer groups. I guess that is why I am highly adaptable to my environments to this day.

Generally, the training we received from our parents helped us to face the world head on.

Seven

COLD-CLIMATE TRAVEL

Northern Roads

Living in the North, you realize that there are many roads less traveled and many non-roads. For example, in Yellowknife there is one highway south, and that's it. Non-roads are really snow machine trails. There aren't a lot of gas stations along the way either. There are also winter ice roads on rivers, lakes, and packed-down stretches of snow that look like roads. The first gas station out of Yellowknife is a three-hour drive. Nearby, there is a bridge over the Mackenzie River.

The 1,510-kilometer drive from Yellowknife to Edmonton, the closest large city in the south, takes about fifteen hours to complete. This explains why, for years, government employees received "isolated-post allowances" on their paychecks for living in Yellowknife or other similar northern communities. The farther north they would go, the bigger the northern allowance. The reasoning: a pound of butter might cost six dollars in Yellowknife, whereas in Ikaahuk, formerly Sachs Harbour, near the Beaufort Sea, butter could cost fifteen dollars a pound.

Seat Sales

There is yet another note in my inbox about another airline's seat sale with a gem: "Don't let the sun set on these spectacular deals." By the time I get around to even opening this e-mail, the sun, moon, and stars would have tumbled and joined a parallel universe. I tend to not open these e-mails until two minutes before they expire, and then I panic. It's a great adrenaline rush. Bookings rarely result from these seat sales in my household.

One reason is that a friend usually needs to be consulted on the timing. This involves resolution of multiple questions: can we both get simultaneous time off work, can our husbands survive without our cooking for a week, can our teenagers possibly be in exams at this time of year, and who will feed the cockatoo? Finally, can we afford this, and is there a better deal out there? Kinda takes the "rush" off the appeal of last-minute travel.

Traveling with Young Children

In the past, traveling with young children could be a challenge. On a seven-hour flight to a southern destination, they would say midflight, "I want to go home now." Once in the big southern city, we would be in search of the stroller-rental place, and after an hour of walking we would still not have found it. We did find a shopping cart. Our son called the stroller a wheelbarrow. On a stopover at Rankin Inlet in Nunavut, one of our sons asked for McDonalds. I tried to explain that the nearest McDonalds would likely be near Montreal.

Rock Band and Burning Ring of Fire

We saw a rock band on one of our trips recently. They were great. There was something up with the lead singer. Someone in the audience had asked the group to play "Superman," and the lead singer told the audience member to "expletive, expletive" in front of the audience. And then he said, "I can't believe I just said that." The lead singer has a great baritone voice. At the end of the concert, the group jammed for one song together with the local band, where they did Johnny Cash's "Ring of Fire." That was awesome! They even had fake smoke coming from under the grand piano.

That song always makes me laugh as it reminds me of one night when we were at the ferry crossing at Fort Providence, which is about a three-hour drive away from Yellowknife. It was close to midnight, pitch black, and the ferry was crashing into the ice like an ice breaker. It appeared that our number might be up that night. It was really tense as we crossed. Ice surrounded the ferry. The ferry kept bumping into it, and we all got really quiet. Then the radio started playing a Johnny Cash song: "I fell into a burning ring of fire, we went down, down, down..." We all started laughing, and that cut the tension. Anyway, hearing that song always reminds me of that night. My husband's cell-phone ring tone is now "Ring of Fire."

Shoparama in the South

For northerners, shopping in the south can be like Christmas. There is more variety and quantity of just about everything. I get a twinkle in my eyes. When shopping with other women, we've been known to postpone supper to shop and then search for a place to eat a hopefully spectacular meal around 9:00 p.m. Due to time constraints while traveling, trying on clothes can be hilarious. One time I got stuck in a dress with my arms straight up. It took some wiggling to get out of it. I was trying on another outfit when I saw a black slicker raincoat. No point in that as it rains infrequently where we live— just snows. I've tried clothes on over other clothes thinking, *Good, if it shrinks in the wash, it will still fit.* One of our best Christmas purchases was toy dogs barking out "Jingle Bells."

We pile all kinds of goodies into our bloated suitcases, which I'm surprised haven't broken the airline weigh scales. One suitcase is jammed with roasts, flat packs of pork chops, hamburger, and the like. Traveling in winter pays off as the meat is already frozen to make the flight back to the North. Another suitcase may be jammed with clothes and vacuum packed. The final suitcase holds books and CDs. Each weighs in at a whopping ninety pounds. Ah, northerners traveling home. We get giddy trying to make the weight limits for each suitcase. If we fail, we start taking items out of the suitcases and reshuffling. It's a rush.

When people who live in the south talk about "going south," they usually mean the Caribbean. When Northerners talk about "going south," they usually mean Edmonton.

Northern Sense of Humor

A northern sense of humor goes something like this. You are driving down the lone highway out of town for a mental break, and the only thing you see for the first fifty kilometers is a crash-test dummy in a hardhat and orange safety vest propped in a lounge chair and waving a flag on the edge of a fifty-foot-high cliff.

The questions you ask yourself upon seeing this sight are as follows: "Will this be the only safety guy I'm going to see for the next 1,510 kilometers?" That is the distance to the next outpost of civilization on this highway. Also, "Who on earth would take the time to dress up a dummy and climb fifty feet up a rocky outcrop to prop him in a chair?"

A rather large German shepherd came bouncing up to the highway edge, which jolted me out of my daze, and I carried on with my drive. Even though I was in the "safety" of a car, I was not taking any chances with the shepherd. It made the dog's day as he puffed up at the end of his driveway in a statuesque pose acting like he had chased away the delinquent car that perchance came close to his imperial domain. The dog stood there in my mirror like an Easter Island figure. Long after he was out of sight, I was sure he was still there, unmoving, looking down the highway in case my car returned.

Pilot in Hotel Elevator

A pilot in a crisp, blue uniform lugging pull-luggage stepped onto the hotel elevator. I asked him if he was working that day. "No, I'm off to the beach," he stated. I said, "Oh!" At another floor, a man got onto the elevator with the pilot and me and asked, "Are you going down?" The pilot responded, "That's not what we pilots want to hear." I said, "Yes, it's like any landing is a good landing." The pilot had a retort for that one too, not missing a beat: "Any *safe* landing is a good landing."

Day of the Dead

To escape the cold weather, there is always the fall or winter vacation. We have now heard forty-eight hours of apparent "no rules" fireworks in Mexico City, *kablampf*. Day of the Dead is the Mexican version of Halloween with more of a religious aspect to it and special traditions over November 1 and 2 to honor people who have passed away. We have seen and heard enough fireworks to wake the dead. Mexico City is alive, and we are not sleeping. It is 25°C at night. It's like being in the middle of a war zone—*boom*, *kablampf*, *kapow*. Their fireworks are not like ours, more like canons going off, really loud, echoing off the volcanoes.

Aztec Sacrifices

An older local man named Nick was our tour guide through a national historic site in Mexico City, and I asked him if the Aztecs only sacrificed women. Nick was a former professor with a deadpan sense of humor. He laughed and said, "Men too—more men than women." I then asked why that was. Nick responded that it was because the men kept asking if they were invited to "the wedding."

Surviving Customs at the Airport

After twelve hours of flying, stopping in multitudinous airports, not smoking for twelve hours, and waiting an hour for our luggage, by the time I hit customs with my declaration form, I gave the agent the flyer's stare, which basically told him, "Here's your form and don't dare ask me one single question. All I have is underwear to declare, which isn't worth declaring, and I need a washroom badly." I placed the form in the customs agent's awaiting hand and walked right through customs, and the back of my body language said, "I am not stopping even if you call me back or send the German shepherds after me." There's something to be said for body language.

Vacation Souvenir

There is a Bobblehead Yoda on my desk, and I use his saber as the holder for my reading glasses. It works for me. It was purchased for the kids on a trip, and not one of them even took it out of the box. So it might as well be a useful desk ornament. It is another toy purchase that will not be wasted.

Oddball Side of Las Vegas

I was thinking about all the oddball things I have seen in Las Vegas, and here's a recap:

- A guy resembling a Vitruvian man who drank too much trying to pass out while standing against a huge metal ball on a statue. He kept sliding down the ball.
- Trying to get a suntan in 100°F.
- The mini Eifel Tower at a store, with the top of it shaped like a private part. I wondered if anyone else had noticed this topper?
- The Mexican musical group who seemed to follow me to every casino where I was camped out at a slot machine. They were at Bally's, Caesars, and Rio for the celebration of Mexican Independence Day. It reminded me of a Mel Brooks movie where an orchestra follows someone around in a bus.
- The lines at some buffets were hysterically long and slow moving. The maîtres d' let the ones with the Premium el Presidente passes in first, so the lines appeared to never move. How do you spell three-dollar pizza slices at another takeout joint, crepes, and three-dollar hot dogs?
- There were brides and grooms everywhere in the casinos, waltzing past the slots in veils matching every conceivable outfit possible, cell-phone cameras a-clicking. One dame tried to convince me that my husband and I should come back to renew our wedding vows with an Elvis impersonator.
- Some actors in costume came cruising through Caesars casino with the lead guy in a Roman uniform

Hairy Leg News

declaring: "All make way for Caesar and his Queen Cleo!" Only in Vegas!

- Walking into the hotel beside Treasure Island, about forty German tourists were all compressed between the two front doors. Then they got the word to go ahead and walk into the hotel. Standing right beside them, I'm thinking the German tourists kind of look like me. I'm sure that I could just "join" them, and they wouldn't even notice. Since they were going to Starbucks, I made a beeline for the casino. It's Tim Hortons for me. Upon telling a Ukrainian woman this story, she said to me, "You must have Ukrainian blood in you." I said, yes, my dad's side of the family. She said, "You think like a Ukrainian." Yes, blend in, join the group, have some fun and laughs, and see where they're going next.

- Magicians Penn and Teller were at the Rio and put on an amazing show. At the beginning of their performance, there was a band playing chamber music with a pianist. Teller "talked" after the show with a whispered "thank-you," and audience members obtained their autographs. What a thrill!

- A film director was in the elevator, and I overheard him saying, "He hasn't read the script yet" with annoyance and sheer frustration showing on his face. I imagined that they were talking about some famous actor. There was a film school conference going on, and all these young people were walking around the casino with film canisters.

- A trade group was holding a convention at the hotel, and when the doors of a conference opened, about two hundred of them were launched directly into the casino—do not pass GO, do not collect two hundred dollars. I was near the doors when they opened and felt like a salmon going upstream.

Another Side of Vegas

Like yin and yang, there is also another side of Vegas:

- Two muggers attacked a sandwich-board guy outside a casino and tried to shove both sides of the sign into the guy. Basically the guy was defenseless. He was OK after the incident but sustained a few bruises. The poor guy was just trying to earn a living.

- Room service at a different hotel was less than stellar. It took an hour to bring food up twenty-six stories, and the entire meal was cold and disgusting—eggs benny with a yellow solid-like sauce, and even the coffee carafe was cold. Maybe it sat there for an hour before it was brought upstairs. I phoned room service to complain—something I rarely do, but this was inedible. The manager said they'd take it off the bill. The American economy was worse than I had thought—even in Vegas. They try to upsell everything. If you buy one slice of pizza, they try to sell you two. If you buy one pop, they try to sell you two and with a free lollipop. Bracelets are billed as *buy three, get three more free*, that kind of thing. If you don't pay attention to all this upselling, you will end up with a suitcase full of items you don't need.

Ice Roads

Another mode of transportation in the North is the ice roads that link communities in winter. During my time as a civil servant and with my newspaper work, I traveled the ice road through the Mackenzie River Delta from Inuvik to Tuktoyaktuk frequently. There are no trees in Tuktoyaktuk since it is above the tree line. The trip amounts to a many-hour drive on ice. Let us just say I put the pickup truck up onto snowbanks just as frequently. Around midafternoon the ice surface gets slick with the sun on it in springtime. This is prime time for doing donuts with your truck whether they were intended or not. Each situation's comic severity was dependent upon many factors: the driver's temperament, how long the driver has been stuck, and when his or her last decent meal was. Once while I was up in a snowbank, a semitrailer came along with an assortment of chains to pull me out. Those are the days you know you're having a good day.

Tourists Visiting Inuvik

Beaufort-Delta residents look forward to the influx of tourists driving the Dempster Highway to Inuvik. The Dempster is a gravel highway starting near Dawson corner, and it goes 456 miles to Inuvik. The edge of the tree line is near Inuvik. Pine and birch trees there are stunted and sparse due to cold temperatures and lack of moisture. Tourists recount stories of driving through forest fires, grizzly bear sightings, and eating dust for breakfast. Even though the trees are sparse, there are still forest fires. Residents refer to it as the "Q-Tip" forest. Tourists also recount following camper drivers who never check their rearview mirrors and drive the same speed as their grandmothers.

It is common to have optical illusions on the highway after driving for long periods. What you thought was a photographer's tripod in the middle of the road was really a caribou. Swerving to avoid ptarmigan finds them swerving with you right into your fender.

Cold-Weather Testing

Seven black Porches pulled up to the local gas pumps the other day when I was gassing up. I thought I was hallucinating as we don't normally see a lot of sports cars up here. We do see a lot of four-by-four pickup trucks. It turned out they were German-speaking drivers up in Yellowknife to do some all-weather testing of their Porches. They shivered in little jackets, and it was -18°C in December. I wonder if we'll see more sports cars up here anytime soon.

Sally the Nervous Flyer

Living in the North, we find that airplanes are our "northern taxis." To get anywhere significant, we often need to fly on small planes. Sally is a nervous flyer. She would lean her head forward against the back of the seat in front of her for take-off. She left one eye open to ensure clouds were still passing by. Sally had flown on Beavers, Twin Otters, and Islanders. The last time she took an Islander, the pilot instructed the passengers to plug their ears because the propellers were so close to the cabin. Another time Sally had to endure no heat in the cabin in winter. It was perishables day. She was planted in a seat behind crates of frozen vegetables. "No quick braking, OK?" Landing at airports is one thing. Airstrips were another.

Sally had landed in all kinds of weather on all kinds of terrain or water. She had experienced short runways, where your neck is left somewhere in San Francisco. She had taken off in zero visibility. She had landed with a cloud ceiling of maybe one hundred feet in ice fog. Nothing had prepared her for a Twin Otter ride to Yellowknife. It had everything the "screamer" roller coaster never had: turbulence, elevator pockets, lightning, thunder, and rain. It was like riding over ocean waves that had frozen mid surf. What really makes flyers nervous is landing—or not landing. The plane was now one hundred feet above the runway. It jerked drastically nose up in fine rocket fashion. The engines gritted their teeth. The plane grunted a thousand times harder than its original design. It ascended at a ninety-degree angle while toilet rolls flipped into the air. Sally's captain said, "Sorry about that, folks. There was another aircraft on the runway." He hoped nobody heard his muffled explanation.

If that's the good news, what is the bad news? The second landing attempt was met by firetrucks following at a distance beside the runway. She was assured by her captain, "This is just a precaution." Someone said they had spotted smoke coming out of the luggage compartment. The plane landed on a postage stamp. Sally was the first in line to disembark the plane— the old washroom trick. After leaving the plane, the passengers were told there had not been a fire. Sally retrieved her luggage and found a two-inch black hole burned into it. When she got home, she phoned her mother, who had loaned her the bag. Yes, that luggage hole was there before she got on the plane.

Murphy's Law on Road Trips

Off on a five-hour drive to another city for the day rather than a "staycation." Things didn't start well. All the gear

Hairy Leg News

was loaded into the new blue truck, and when we went to start it—*click, click*. The starter was dead. So everything was hauled out and put into another truck, the green truck.

It reminded me of the time our entire family piled into the green truck at 8:00 a.m. in a hotel parking lot in the middle of nowhere, and I said to everyone, "Wow, it's great to get off to an early start." *Click, click*. The starter was dead. This meant calling a tow truck, gassing up, and pushing the truck from the gas station to the repair shop. These events only happen on weekends. We were very fortunate to find one mechanic in town who was able to fix it some six hours later. Yep, off to an "early start."

Another early start was when my brother and I piled into his racing car to drive to a small village about three hours away. We stopped for lunch at a huge shopping mall, where someone pointed out that our gas tank was hanging by a single strap. Some six hours later, again on a Saturday, we found the one person in town who could fix it. There were well-meaning suggestions of maybe we should be taking the train. We just drove back home when it was fixed. Did I mention we also got lost?

What's an NWT sandwich? It's a sandwich with tread marks on it from racing to the next gas station near the NWT-Alberta border before the next gas station closes.

Northern Road Trips

Not everyone living in the western Arctic chooses to fly for their holidays. Some northerners choose the family drive and camping summer vacation. When there's one highway out of town, you quickly learn to multitask for the long road trip.

This includes the following:

- Fish in the cooler for drinks while doing Search-A-Word puzzles.
- Find a radio station that isn't country music and glance at newspaper headlines.
- Wash bugs from the windshield and bumpers while dodging a rather large bumblebee and horse flies.
- Batting bugs out of the windows while applying Bug Out! to bug bites.
- Scanning a bison herd for movement while searching the hotel guides.
- Wiping the picnic table while making a four-course gourmet meal of dinosaur noodles, boiled-bag rice, fried Spam, and toasted day-old bread.

Northern Suitcases

It is common knowledge that northerners leave with many empty suitcases and come back north with bulging luggage. Once I packed a suitcase, and there was music inside the suitcase when I returned home. I unpacked it and found one of my son's handheld computer games crushed against a teapot.

Northerners bring back an abundance of food and other items that either can't be found where they live or are in short supply. This includes Montreal smoked meat and bagels, pastries, and specialty foods. Curtains and bedding are other items where there are more choices online or in the south. I once brought an entire suitcase filled with boxed grape juice all the way from Edmonton to Inuvik, and lifting the suitcase to put it onto the weigh scale gave us tennis elbow for a week.

My friend Sally likes to vacuum pack everything in her suitcase. She borrows the vacuum cleaner from the hotel and does an incredible job of getting five stacks into one. Sally sits on the suitcase and zips it up around her. Works like a charm.

On one vacation, my suitcase was on a carousel behind 258 pieces of luggage from a tour company. The conveyor belt creaked. A fellow Canadian who was still waiting for his luggage to appear remarked, "Let's crack open a bottle of rye and have a few belts." The final suitcase to appear was the only one with straps. It was wide open, straps dangling and gauzy, pale apricot lingerie clinging to the outside. No one claimed it. No one wanted to claim it. At this point the luggage handler told us to move to the next room. A Jeep shot up to the carousel. It braked. The luggage lunged forward then jerked back. Some fell off. This luggage was meant for the group behind us.

A bus quickly took me to my hotel. There was not the oceanfront view that was anticipated. It was a stagnant pond at the back of the hotel. No fishing there. Good for stick dunking. I decided to search for the hotel's restaurant. I could not find it. I sheepishly went to the front desk. It turned out the restaurant was outside on the pool deck. I come from a place where the majority of restaurants are inside the building. It never occurred to me that it would be outside. I decided that I have lived in the North too long and needed to get out more often.

Vehicles in Winter

After decades of cold-weather living, I have developed a sick sense of humor. It was -57°C with a wind chill. The car had been plugged in overnight, and it was so cold that the two extension cords were stuck together. They also appeared to have shrunk. I finally pried them apart and tried to start the engine. Miraculously and after crying "thank God!" several times, it started. The radio switched on, and the first song that hit my ears was "California Girls" by the Beach Boys. I drove past snowplows, snowbanks, and

Hairy Leg News

tow trucks while hearing that the surf was up, "and the northern girls with the way they kiss, they keep their boy-friends warm at night...Wish they all could be California girls."

One severely icy day, a neighbor's vehicle would not start. Out came the jumper cables and then the battery charger to recharge the battery. If that didn't do it, the battery would be disconnected and brought into the house to warm up.

If anyone in town can get their vehicle going in this weather, they are likely to then run out of gas after idling the car too long to warm it up.

One of my favorite winter songs is "Beverly Hills—that's where I wanna be..." I let my imagination take me to palm-tree-lined medians, open blue skies, and Rodeo Drive.

Driving Ice Cubes on Wheels

People start their cars in -40°C and can be seen driving their frozen ice cubes on square or flat tires. Their windows are all fogged up, and they are scraping the insides of the front win-dows. The heat is turned up full blast, and the radio is on full blast too. They slowly back out of their driveways and pro-ceed down the road. To someone watching them, the drivers look like they are in an enclosed sauna on wheels.

The eastern side of Canada once had a record-breaking dump of snow measuring forty-eight centimeters. Montreal got it especially bad. If you've been caught in one of those snow bonanzas, you may have stopped at an aunt's house or a farmhouse overnight.

In the morning, I shoveled four feet of snow from around my car. Gazing down the road, I saw the mounds of snow-banked cars stuck up like haphazard moguls on a prairie ski hill. The buried cars looked like sticky buns or marshmallows with only their side mirrors sticking out from beneath the snow. Drivers warmed up their cars for an hour or so and hoped the graders would show up and clear the roads. My only fear at this point was that there would be another dump of snow or that a grader would hem me in behind a snow-bank before I could get going.

Winter Getaways

Hardy winter enthusiasts still like to head south for warmer climates. Similarly, southerners like to have northern holidays at ski lodges. It is human nature to want what we do not have at hand. So every year about a million Canadian snowbirds head to Mexico. Others go the Florida or commute to other southern American states. Some lock up their houses for winter or get house sitters. Others choose to live in condos, so it is not a big deal to leave town for five and a half months a year while still maintaining their Canadian healthcare coverage.

Some locations have adapted to Canadians coming south in wintertime. They actually serve poutine in some parts of Florida, recognizing the strong presence of French Canadians there.

One Mexican house sitter swapped his Mexican home for one in Montreal, Canada, in wintertime. He said he only went outside for groceries or to shovel snow, and it cured him of ever wanting to come back in the wintertime. I think the Canadian got the better end of that deal.

Multilingual Animals

Animals can be unilingual or multilingual. While watching several Mexican dogs on a rooftop, I said *hi* to them, and nothing registered. I then said *hola*, and they responded. Then it occurred to me that those dogs only understand Spanish. For example, my friend's cat is bilingual and understands "meeenooou" and "cat."

I pictured all these international dogs barking in the cargo hold of a plane and someone telling them, "Be quiet!" But only some would understand as they could understand only their masters' language. Like the German dogs would only understand "*rouste*!"

Dog obedience school would be really screwed up if it were international. You would need interpreters. Plus the dogs would be used to their own country's food, not our North American diet.

I heard of one fellow who was worried about his dogs being snatched, so he gave them commands only in German. He figured if someone took the dogs, at least they wouldn't understand English commands.

Camparama and High Winds

The weather forecast for the weekend was ninety-kilometer winds all two days. But our friends had already booked several campsites, so they decided to go anyway. They came back at 3:00 a.m. soaked and shivering. Their tents collapsed in the wind and rain, and their blankets were full of water. We were supposed to go up to see them at the campsite but opted for a nice warm house instead, watching *Auntie Mame* with Rosalind Russell. It's Murphy's Law: plan camparama and bring on torrential rainfall.

Drivers' Wish List for Manufacturers

The Canadian cold-weather drivers' wish list for car manufacturers includes better heated windshield wipers such as something you'd see on a Sherman tank; heaters that work like direct-fired, infrared Herman Nelsons; and tires with three-inch treads.

The defrost feature would include the entire car—defrosting windows, doors, door handles, key locks, hoods, and trunks. There would be mandatory heated seats plus hot-air vents in the ceiling and the interior's sides.

Tires would be designed with deflation prevention for fluctuating temperatures. Tire valves would be at least an inch in circumference so they could be seen on a dark day in January. Also, idling time would not be required for vehicle warm-ups since engines would have a built-in warming blanket similar to a horse blanket. I'm not sure how this works though with the gas mix.

White paint would not be an option for car exteriors as white cars become invisible in snowbanks. Car colors would be offered in ranges of neon. Metal spikes would spring out of the tires at the push of a button for driving on black ice like a James Bond car.

There would be emergency light signals on the front, back, and sides of the car. If anyone has drifted into a 360-degree spin on black ice in the dark or in fog, that person would understand this desire. And—this has nothing to do with winter—a special place for a purse between the front seats would bedazzle most women.

Drive-Thru Black Ice

There was recently a huge snow dump here of one foot of snow on top of black ice. When my brother was going through a drive-thru for a coffee, he drove up to the window and said in his mellow, low voice, "He-lllooooh, laaadies." And then, as his car slid past the window, "Gooood-byyyyye, laaadies." He had to go all the way around the building again and back through the line. He was laughing the whole time.

My brother also recalled that one time all of the people in the drive-thru line had to get out of their cars to push the guy at the top of the line after his car died as he got his order. Everyone pushing was teasing the driver. It must have been embarrassing, but this sounded to me like another great excuse for being late for work.

Drive-Thru Communications

Today I ordered myself a coffee at the drive-thru, paid for it, and went to get groceries. After loading the groceries into the car, I reached for my coffee, but it wasn't there. I had forgotten to pick it up at the drive-thru window. When I went back to the drive-thru, they were laughing that they were just about to hand it to me through the window and saw me speeding off.

Recently, we went through a hamburger outlet's drive-thru. They had put in a new speaker system with two rows instead of one for cars to go through. The first time we went there, the attendant couldn't hear a thing:

"Two grilled cheese," I said.

"Whhhhhaaaaaaaaaaat?"

"Two grilled cheese."

"Whaaaat?"

"Two grilled cheese."

"Whaaat?"

Then I stepped on the gas, passed the speaker, and heard, "Do you want ketchup with that?"

I had to yell from three cars up, "Noooooooooooooo ketchup."

Well, last night I went through with my free fries voucher. "I'd like a free fry and nothing else, thank you."

"Is that everything?"

"Yep, that's it."

"Is that everything?"

"Yep, that's everything."

"Is that everything?"

"Nothing else!"

Then varooooom to the first window to drop off the voucher. Then varrrrrrrrooooooooooom to the second window, where attendants were laughing their heads off. Then varoooooooom, outta there.

This reminded me of the time we went to a different drive-thru for snacks. The squawk box had wires hanging out of it as if it had been hit the night before by a Mack truck. But it still worked. We just talked into the wires.

Another time a note was posted on the advertising display sign that read, "Do not order here." Some people were confusing the advertising display with the order squawk box.

The best was when a donut shop ran out of donuts and posted a sign: "No donuts." It must have been highly embarrassing for them at the very least, this being a "donut" shop. Apparently it was a high-demand weekend for donuts.

Squawk Box Hilarity

Passing through a fast-food drive-thru this morning, I drove around a vertical driller with five pickup trucks around it looking as if they were drilling for diamonds right in the parking lot. Then we got to the speaker, where they had a portable car speaker hung over the regular squawk box with a sign that read, "Turn off vehicle to order." The portable speaker looked like something from the recycling bin, like the kind of thing somebody would rig up with old wire hangers. Priceless! I t was hard to stop laughing long enough to order. I got to the attendant and said, "Oh, I see you have a new speaker!" She said, "Ya, we're so technologically advanced here. I think the building is going to cave in on us." I should've had my camera.

Things to Do in Line at the Drive-Thru

The drive-thru lineup was taking far too long the other day. Someone must have been ordering for the entire hockey team. Fortunately, I have compiled a list of things to do in the drive-thru lineup: count pennies; unravel braids; dab on lipstick or mascara; turn the volume on the stereo up or down, depending on proximity to the speaker; look at the entire menu on the order board, noting all the things you never order because they are too healthy or involve lettuce; deal out a hand of rummy or Texas hold 'em.

Police Chase

It used to be we would get excited when the latest video rental came to town. I would hop into my car and go barreling down the highway to get there before all the copies were rented out. One day on my way back home, a police car pulled me over for speeding on the highway.

The officer asked me why I was speeding. My reply was, "The new *McHale's Navy* video rental just came in, and I just had to get it. You know the one where retired Lieutenant Commander Quinton McHale spends his days putzing around the Caribbean in an old PT-73 selling homebrew."

The police officer shook his head, eyes gazing down at the video on the seat beside me, and his mouth formed a mini smirk as he muttered in a low voice, "I haven't heard that one before." He let me go with a warning.

Another time I was caught speeding while running late for taking my son to the family doctor. That time I did get a ticket. So now I get it. For something totally inconsequential,

I don't get a ticket. For something important, I get a ticket. That's life!

Illuminated *Fasten Seat Belt* Sign

After shoparama, I kept chucking things into my purse like door and window catalogues, and it got so heavy that the "fasten seat belt" sign came on when the purse landed on the front seat. It took me a while to figure out that blinking light, along with the passenger-side airbag light. But the same thing happened once when I bounced a frozen turkey onto the front seat—it needed a seatbelt.

Eight

BOREDOM ABOVE THE SIXTY-SECOND PARALLEL

Cabin Fever

My daily horoscope for January 29: "You feel a bit of cabin fever and are restless so make sure you have an outlet for these pent-up feelings." Yes, it's called snow shoveling and watching hockey.

Types of Snow and Ice

People are so bored in winter that they categorize the snow. There's crystal, sparkly snow; sticky, sushi-rice, clingy, snowball-making snow; dusty snow; yellow snow; and wet, heavy, do-not-want-to-shovel snow. There are also different types of ice: candling ice, cracked ice, solid ice, one-foot-thick ice, spring-breakup ice, and not-for-cocktails ice or dirty ice.

Nickname Generator

There's an online nickname generator, so I plugged in my name and got "Noodle Glitzy" and "Nanny Goober." I think I prefer Nancearoonie.

Bored with Winter

Numb-with-boredom individuals can also look at the statistics for the number of Canadian tree farms and the number of hectares used to grow Christmas trees in Canada. Or they may prefer to read about the nice weather in Fiji.

If people are really bored, they can look up the average mean temperature for January or February. Our average, with wind chill, is about -57°C for those two months, according to my own personal calculations. Although I'm sure the weather gurus will tell us it's much warmer than that, such as -30°C.

The only reasons to go outside when it is that cold are few: Christmas parties, grocery shopping, work, driving kids around, and, of course, more shoveling.

Other pastimes for the bored are board games, online games, researching the pyramids, taking out the recycling or garbage, decluttering, or shoveling some more. Then there's hibernating with a good book, eating, and sleeping.

If you really want to challenge yourself, go outside to the cold storage shed in the dark to try to find another rock-hard extension cord for the car or the Christmas tree. There's a good chance you will just go to the local box store and buy another one. In the summertime, you will walk into the shed and wonder why you have a dozen extension cords that aren't being used.

Another pastime is building a snowman or two if the snow is sticky. In spring the snowmen melt either limbo style or vertically until it's just the head and hat embedded in more snow.

Things to Do in Winter When Bored

Women can do many things in winter when bored with hibernation. Making ice candles is a great pastime. It's easy to do. Place water into a bucket, leaving about three inches at the top. Place it outside in -57°C for about twenty-four hours. Bring it inside until the edges melt and then slide it out. Bring it back outside and insert a candle or Christmas lights. Voila—ice candles.

Puzzles and games are other diversions. There is an online game where we click on three gems in a row, and if we are really good at it, they catch fire. Or, while shoveling, we scan the driveway for tracks of foxes, ravens, or doggies. When really bored, there is a two-day tourtière recipe to try out.

Things to Do in Winter—Habitual Vacuuming

Vacuuming behind the couch uncovered a nest of dust and a whole family of sparrows that had moved in. Washing the floor behind the couch in the living room and vacuuming under the cushions revealed a treasure trove of forty cents in change, a fifty-cent Canadian Tire money bill, and—the jackpot—a Christmas cracker, which was broken to reveal a can opener for a posthausfrau beer that I'm about to crack open.

One time, I was vacuuming too close to the toilet paper dispenser. The bottom of the toilet paper was dangling lower than usual. The vacuum sucked up the end of the toilet paper and it kept going and going. By the time I punched the off button, there was nothing left on the toilet paper roll.

Winternet

Since there is not a lot to do outside when it's -40°C, a lot of people surf the "Winternet." A great amount of time is spent on this godsend looking up ridiculous things such as the lyrics to "In a Gadda Da Vida," the cooking time for range chickens, and how to recognize a tropical beach.

Ponderings

- How do you know when your roll of invisible tape has run out?
- Why is the Mayan god Chac Mool never seen standing up, and why does he have a TV tray on his stomach?
- Why is it when you break something you have the least amount of money to fix it?
- Why do Christmas lights always get snarled after you put them away neatly in a box?

UFO TV Show and Space Shuttle

There was this TV show on UFOs the other night. They displayed this artifact that they found in Mexico and claimed it was a replica of the space shuttle, which had traveled fifteen hundred years back in time—yes, time travel—to the Mayans, who then made this artifact of the space shuttle. To me the artifact looked like a ten-cent fishing lure. Then they said they would make a replica of the artifact and see if it flew, which it did, just like the space shuttle. How did they come up with that one?

Maybe there's more scientific basis to this than we know; maybe we do not know everything. Or maybe this show should be canceled.

Fireball Sighting

On February 4, 2009, a fireball low in the sky and parallel to the earth near Yellowknife burned up in the atmosphere. Wondering what it was, I decided to contact Environment Canada. The standard response is as follows:

> *We have no expertise or information on fireballs, but I suggest you inquire with or report your sightings to these folks: Natural Resources Canada, Meteorites and Impacts Advisory Committee (MIAC), or SpaceWeather.*
>
> *Yours truly,*
> *Meteorological Guru*

Yep, they believe me. Sure…

Odd 911 Calls

There was an item on the news about unusual 911 calls. The two that caught my attention were the squirrel acting suspiciously and the snapping turtle that the caller was afraid would leap into moving traffic.

I have never seen a suspicious-looking squirrel, but I could visualize one. It would have had big, round brown eyes, a prominent forehead, beaver teeth, spiky hair, and an elongated tail. Its modus operandi would be putting ear to wire and listening in on telephone landlines. Or running up a pole into the birdhouse.

The snapping turtle jumping into oncoming traffic is a little tougher to visualize as justifying a 911 call unless it was on some kind of steroid.

Society Columnist

One urban legend recounted that there once was a society columnist working for the media who wrote up birthday greetings for people who had been dead for two years or more. Seriously? Another urban legend?

William and Kate

Prince William and Kate, the Duke and Duchess of Cambridge, came to Yellowknife in July 2011. My employer gave me time off work to see the event. Let's just say I was pressed up against a fence for the better part of a morning as part of the fan paparazzi trying to get photos. I now have a picture of the couple with a large hat in front of their faces and another with a large, extended hand front and center. Let's just say we'll leave the photography to the professionals.

Useless Information

Every day we are bombarded with useless information. A recent e-mail of factoids will attest to this:

- Mickey Mouse is known as "Topolino" in Italy. Great, I'll remember this if ever visiting Italy again.
- The letter *J* does not appear anywhere on the periodic table of the elements. Where was this gem when I was kicked out of chemistry class after two weeks in grade eleven?
- In 2012, December has five Fridays, five Saturdays, and five Sundays. This apparently happens once every 823 years and is called "money bags." I guess the money is from having five weeks to save up to pay the rent or mortgage.
- Other useless information includes weather forecasts for a week when you know a lot can change in a day and how to repair a span bridge with duct tape or cello wrap.

Baba O'Riley

I am singing the words to The Who's "Baba O'Riley," and I have changed the words as I'm singing from "before we get much older" to "before we get much colder" as I am driving and cranking up the heat in my fogged-up car destined for the grocery store. For the next song, my CD player display panel lights up with: "Life's Been Goo" as it cannot display the entire title of the Joe Walsh song: "Life's Been Good." The Beach Boys' "California Girls" just started playing on my CD player. This always rates a smirk in the frigid temperatures. If it is too cold, the CDs won't play. This must be a good day in the Arctic.

Cave Dwellers

I am brushing my teeth, pondering what the early cavemen used prior to the invention of toothbrushes. Pine gum and twigs for toothpicks? Who knows? If I am really bored, I will Google it. It seems it was their natural diets.

NHL Lockout

Another saving-grace item for surviving the long winters is watching sports on television. Watching hockey is a national pastime. I admit it: I am a female sports fan.

On Day 111 of no hockey due to an NHL lockout, the NHL Players Association and owners negotiated a tentative new labor agreement.

No NHL hockey? Our football season had ended at the tail end of November. It was now January. OK, so sports fans have been able to catch up on curling, junior world hockey,

Hairy Leg News

and skiing. In addition, they have been able to get to household tasks they never had time for before. My husband even put up a new porch light.

Defeating all stereotypes, in my all-male household not one of the boys likes hockey except maybe in the playoffs, since they are computer geeks. I am the sole year-round hockey and football fan on the home front.

My first inkling of this was when one of my sons said he had never seen an "expedition game." Er, yeah, that's "exhibition game." They also thought there were four quarters in hockey until their eighth birthdays.

During the NHL lockout, when pro hockey in North America pretty much ceased to exist, it did not affect my sons' day-to-day lives at all. For me, there was the world juniors' tournament as an alternative to NHL hockey deprivation. It did affect my free time big time. In order to see a "live" game, I would have to haul myself out of bed at 2:00 a.m. or 4:00 a.m. to watch hockey in a different time zone.

I ended up writing this book to fill in the hours wasted waiting for pro hockey to return. I also managed to finally shave my legs in midwinter, dramatically reducing my resemblance to Sasquatch.

One inventive hockey player during the NHL lock-out had a TV endorsement where he served up a pizza on the flat side of a hockey stick as the pizza came sizzling out of the oven. It reminded me of the times my brother would melt a plastic blade onto the shaft of his broken hockey sticks to fix them. This would extend the life of his sticks.

A food shop in Nunavut reported it wasn't selling as many pizzas during the lockout. This must have affected pizza outlets nationwide.

I have not heard the words "he shoots; he scores!" in six months now.

When NHL hockey does return to the screen, the only differences the guys in my household will notice will be the commercials and the ends of the games, when they can switch the channel to *Dr. Who*. Canada with no hockey is un-thinkable to me.

Don Cherry, Fashionista

In addition to no NHL hockey during the strike, a favorite CBC TV sports commentator of mine, Don Cherry, was also quiet. Quiet? I missed seeing the sports fashionista's zany suits. I also missed his commentaries on *Coach's Corner*.

What was Don doing in his spare time? Maybe he was shoveling his driveway, although I did hear on the news that he was helping out with scouting prospects for the Ontario Hockey League. It's nice to know Don Cherry stayed active in the hockey world, and I was relieved to see him back on *Coach's Corner*. Actually, I missed Don Cherry's commentaries more than I missed the NHL hockey games.

Kids and adults continued to play hockey. They went to practice at 5:00 a.m., when you could see your breath inside the frigid rink; they played road hockey *interruptus*, interspersed with "Car!" And seniors played hockey around midnight, when they could get the ice time. The pros must have been busy playing snow golf, making commercials, or practicing table hockey at home.

If I Could Be a Hockey Commentator

It would be fun to be a hockey commentator. If I had the chance, I would add bad poetry to the mix to brighten up the dialogue with something like this:

It's over the glass
He fell on his ass
Shots in the period
They were a myriad
Point shot—he scored

And the crowd roared
The organist played AC/DC
It's time for a brewskie.

Gordie Howe—Mr. Hockey

Gordie Howe, aka Mr. Hockey, Detroit's infamous number nine, was in Yellowknife for a fundraiser for the slain peace officers fund. They held a police-firefighters hockey game with Gordie and his son Marty in attendance. It was nice that they could come up for that fundraiser. It meant a lot to a lot of people.

Oilers Game

I heard one of the Oilers games was a doozy, and they were throwing pizza boxes on the ice in disgust when an Oilers goal was disallowed. I guess Don Cherry gave a player on the winning team heck for showboating after scoring a goal. But to put it in context, it was a doozy game, and they were all excited. I figure as long as a player's not doing cartwheels on skates, it should be OK.

Arguing with the Ref

I grew up watching sports with my father and brother, so I joined them and became an armchair quarterback too.

If the ref made a call we deemed unworthy, we would all pipe up, "Didn't he see that?" What we really wanted was to argue with the ref: "Are you sure about that call? Do you not recognize interference when you see it?" Similar for hockey: "Uh, the guy from the other team was sprawled across the goalie. How could the goalie possibly stop the puck? That's goalie interference. How could you not see that?"

Of course, nowadays, with refs viewing instant replays, the calls are more accurate. While technology is great, the referee reviews of potential penalties have also slowed the pace of the games.

Boredom

There isn't much to do up North that we haven't done. We've worked freelance contracts and traveled. Today for entertainment I picked some Saskatoon berries from our front yard. Wow, the excitement never ends. I did two loads of laundry and then didn't know what to do next. So I made lasagna for supper, picked more berries, sat on the deck, and swatted insects. It felt like my neighbors and I were the first bunch of women who came North and wanted to get out of town for a break, but the only way out was by dog team. In our case, there is one highway to the south.

Music Documentary

We were watching a documentary about The Wrecking Crew. These musicians played in the 1960s for many bands, including the Beach Boys. One of the lead musicians, Tommy Tedesco, said he disliked his day job so much that he practiced playing the guitar every day. Thank you, Tommy Tedesco, for giving me the inspiration many years ago to keep writing.

Lightning Storm

Some days small-town life in Yellowknife can be about making our own fun. So my neighbors came over, and we drank beer until 4:00 a.m. while watching a seven-hour lightning storm. We sat out on lawn chairs in the warm rain. We were rating each lightning strike as one would rate a springboard diver in the Olympics: 7.1, 5.2, et cetera. Some people know how to have way too much fun. Then I started taking Andy Warhol–style photos of the neighbors watching spider web lightning. We must be really hard up for entertainment.

Northern Ways to Procrastinate—or How to Aggravate Yourself

- Call up a research company and ask for northern statistics on anything. Wait twenty minutes. Someone will come back on the line and explain there are almost no statistics kept on northern Canada.

Hairy Leg News

- Book a flight during fog or blizzard season.
- Book a helicopter flight during forest fire season.
- Book a flight to a small community where everything is closed including the sole motel. Grab a pebble and try hitting the cook's window thirty feet up.
- Take a motorboat down the Mackenzie River channel and get lost. Stop the engine and find you cannot restart it. Start swatting jumbo mosquitos with the oars. Be sure to miss your friend with the oars.
- Try opening a car door after a bout of freezing rain.
- Try putting all your baking in the shed outside only to discover a fox or raven ate it all.
- Look up the meaning of "dictionary" in the dictionary.

Nine

HOLIDAYS NEAR THE ARCTIC CIRCLE

White Christmas

Canadian winter allows for traditions to carry on, such as the "snow-white Christmas" custom of finding a tree and decorating it for the ho-ho-holiday. It could be a live tree or an artificial one. "Southern" Christmas trees can be purchased from the local Boy Scouts. Christmas tree varieties in Yellowknife are spruce and pine. According to Statistics Canada, our country exports Christmas trees worth millions. The trick is getting the lights on with the baubles and leaving the tree still standing upright. A child running the tinsel around the tree finishes the job.

Northern Christmas Trees

When one is searching in the boreal forest for a northern Christmas tree, it is common to find 120-year-old black spruce trees that are six feet high. It takes so long to grow them due to the terrain, weather, and lack of moisture. So northerners often feel guilty cutting down those trees because it took them so long to grow. Imagine the history they've seen in their lifetimes. We drag them home in the back of pickup trucks or on snowmobile sleds and let them rest in the house. When we get them up, the use of zip ties helps secure them in place. The branches are sparse. Placing a heavy decoration on the tree will result in the branch sagging six inches. So we have a lot of lighter-weight ornaments. The last time we adorned the Christmas tree with an angel on top, the angel looked like it was on a dive tower leaning forward on a forty-five-degree angle about to do a triple gainer.

Oh, Christmas Tree

On the drive into work this dark morning, in a half-awake haze, I saw that there appeared to be a Christmas tree moving along the sidewalk. It was a jogger with flashing red lights in an inverted triangle on his backpack. Funny how the brain associated that with a Christmas tree. Bring on more coffee.

Christmas Lights

It's a great idea to plug in Christmas lights in October before the cords freeze in one position and get covered in several feet of snow. Chances are the extension cords will stay in that position all winter. Two vans just drove by, one with Christmas lights lit up inside the van. The other van had glowing Christmas lights around the top, serpentine style around Tim Hortons' takeout coffee cups. I think the cups were secured by ice as they did not move despite the van going fast.

Christmas Lights and Prongs

Of course, with Christmas lights, it is always something. I went to plug the extension cord into the socket on the front porch and discovered it was for a two-pronged plug—say that fast ten times: "two-pronged prug." All our cords have three prongs. So off I went to the local hardware store.

They had something that plugs into the two-prong socket, and the other side is three-prong. Who knew? Perfect. Hooked that up and then went back to the shed to get the extension cord. It just made it to the deck, not an inch to spare. The Christmas lights are now along the front of the deck, and they lit up! I am a firm believer that extension cords for the North should be in the thousand-foot lengths.

Hanging Christmas Lights

Due to the fact that we can get -57°C with the wind chill in winter, many people choose to put their Christmas lights up in, let's say, June. This is a much more pleasant experience than standing in snowy boots on a slick chair, trying to hang Christmas lights on the porch in winter.

In the good old days, if one bulb didn't work, the entire string of lights didn't work. The most consecutive swear words that I ever heard from my father came out when he was on a twelve-foot frozen metal ladder replacing burned-out bulbs along the rooftop with his bare hands and no one holding the ladder. I could hear the rattling and shaking of the ladder, and he refused any help. In those days apparently it was a sign of weakness to ask for help.

I put my outside Christmas lights up on the weekend. I was on a ladder in front of the front door, and my big fear was that my husband would forget that I was out there, open the front door, and send me flying into a snowbank in a backward swan dive, still clutching the lights. I always announce I'm going out there to do the lights before I set foot on the ladder.

Note to self: wet snow on boots and a wooden kitchen chair are not a prudent alternative to getting out the ladder.

Bad Glass
Our Santa Claus snowman glass globe broke while I was loading it into the dishwasher. Apparently I missed some vacuuming it up because a piece became embedded in the

bottom of my foot. It just happened to be 5:00 a.m., so I was being really quiet about it: "Aaaaaaaaaaaaaaaah!"

Yellowknife Golf Course

In the summertime, Yellowknifers have a nine-hole golf course for entertainment. Locals joke that the ravens steal their balls. They also joke there that the greens are really the rough. People bring their own short-pile synthetic turf to hit the balls on the tee-offs as the course is mostly sand. There is also a tourist draw with the Midnight Sun Golf Tournament. In November and during Christmas holidays, the area near the course is replaced by cross-country skiing.

Vehicles on Christmas Day

When you wake up on Christmas day and it is frigid temperatures, the extension cord to your block heater and car battery becomes an umbilical lifeline. You try to very slowly roll down the electric windows, which are covered in ice and snow. You try the windshield wipers, which have formed a frozen arc, and the rubber doesn't even touch the windshield. Of course, you are out of washer fluid. The best is when the cord plug gets stuck to the car cord and you can't budge it. If the power goes out, you are really hooped. This is a good day to stay put.

Christmas Visit

Our sons came home for the Christmas holidays, so we now have four grown males in the household again. I am starting to feel like Sasquatch as I cannot get near the bathroom for all the showers, shaving, and primping. Twenty sweaty towels in various states of fraying and decay are flung onto the bathroom racks. I am starting to feel like I walked into a decrepit archaeological dig site. This reminds me, I must get a new set of bathroom towels.

Watching young men decorating a Christmas tree is like watching fireflies whizzing around a mulberry bush. It is a flurry blur of bodies flitting in and out of the living room to the basement, bathroom, and kitchen. A whirl of lights wind around the tree as if jet propelled and randomly razzle-dazzle the ends of branches, while ornaments are strewn about like confetti landing on newlyweds. The now fully grown boys finally admit they do not want to decorate the tree. I had not noticed. In the family album, the tree-decorating pictures are digital swooshes because the boys move like drones on steroids.

Other signs that I am in an all-male household again include the way the hinges on the fridge squeak, the freezer door no longer stays closed, and food disappears after midnight.

It felt like my husband and I worked in a cafeteria. For a solid week, we lived in the kitchen; we started to watch TV in there and read our newspapers while waiting on food in the oven. I took to filing my nails and completed a two-thousand-hour online computer course while waiting for food to cook.

We made homemade egg muffins, tourtières, turkey, ham, macaroni and cheese, pizza, stuffed eggplant, spaghetti, chicken fingers, dozens of cookies, tarts, and chocolate logs.

The dishwasher was constantly thrashing. There was a certain hum to the household when the boys visited—the hum of, "Hmm, where is that block of cheese that I put into the fridge, and where is that case of soda pop I just brought home from the grocery store?" Once again, I am best friends with the grocery store cashiers as we are there daily. I now totally understand why Erma Bombeck hid food such as chocolate cake in obscure places.

This year we decided to make popcorn balls with jujubes. Even though we greased our hands, we were sticking to everything: the spoon, the pot, and the popcorn balls. At one point we called out for help to get unstuck from the melted marshmallow clumps. I firmly believe this recipe requires grandparents to be present. It was a triumph to get the batch onto a cookie sheet and into the fridge to set for five minutes. When the boys left to go south again for college and work, my husband was the first to notice that the fridge handle was broken.

Doomsday Predictions

My definition of an optimist is someone who buys Christmas wrapping paper on sale on Boxing Day despite the doomsday predictors forecasting that the world will end four days before Christmas next year.

Box Store Public Address System

In a box store during the pre-Christmas hysteria, shoppers heard the following announcement on the public address system: "Attention, shoppers, there's a blue pickup truck in the parking lot with food in the back. The ravens are going at it." A wave of chuckles rolled from one department to another all the way through the store. My teenage son—on an emergency pajama run in the men's apparel section—was thought to be the truck owner, but indeed it was not him.

Green-Lantern Christmas

One season, Sally's son worked as a cashier at a grocery store. He even wore a Santa hat. The next year staff members were told that they could wear red or green T-shirts so long as there were no words printed on them. He appeared at the cash register as the Green Lantern comic-book character, taking staff dress codes to new heights.

Christmas Mixed Messages

One Christmas Sally was given a book about how to lose weight with the subliminal message, "for tomorrow you shall die." She also received a box of chocolates. Yes, losing weight while chomping down on bonbons is my kind of diet. Sign me up!

Christmas Power Walker and Dog

A woman was power walking her dog, rushing the dog along as she didn't want to break her exercise stride. So I wished her a merry Christmas, and she carried on in a big hurry, power walking her dog along until they got two doors away, where the dog stopped, laid his butt into the snow, and started having a poop. She had to wait for him, which broke her stride. So, I was thinking to myself, *Oh, he's having a power poop.*

Christmas Package in July

They had a "scare" at the airport today. Someone left a wrapped Christmas gift outside. They closed the airport, all the staff shuffled outside, and a group of police officers closed in on the package. I don't know if the police blew it up, but the surprise package was a home steam cleaner. Someone will be out a Christmas present.

Only in Yellowknife

In Yellowknife we have an expression that we use constantly: "Only in Yellowknife." This can refer to just about anything that people can retell in terms of oddball, madcap stories or things that people seem to get away with that they wouldn't anywhere else. The stories are strange or difficult to imagine but resonate with reality because no one could have made them up.

Our friend Fred told us that one morning after he and his wife had gone to a Christmas party, he woke up to find a stranger sleeping on his couch. They'd left their friend at home watching TV the night before. They asked him who the guy was, but he did not know him either. So Fred woke him up and asked what he was doing there on his couch. It ended up this guy had been at a party in the neighborhood and had let himself into the wrong house and crashed on the couch. He was really embarrassed and went home, and then a few days later he sent Fred a gift with a thank-you note.

The Gold Range is a Yellowknife bar known by locals as Sam's Bar or the "Strange Range." Over the years the Gold

Range had acquired a reputation for wild chair-flying fights like something out of the Wild West. On the restaurant side, where stir fry is a popular item, a sign reads, "You want more pork, you order pork chops!" In the past, the Range bar has hosted a Saturday afternoon amateur hour, when people would amble up the stage and start singing. It was like karaoke without people knowing the actual words to the songs, and it was great entertainment.

The Gingerbread House

Once upon a time in a faraway place in the North, there lived a woman who had never made a gingerbread house. *My goodness*, she thought, *it's about time I made one.*

Directing my sabotaged grocery cart down the aisles, one wheel slightly off, I mulled over who might have last used this cart to move an entire household's effects, including the baby grand piano. I chose the gingerbread kit with everything included. At home, I pulled into the driveway, mesmerized by our new marquee of synchronized Christmas lights.

The kit sat for two weeks until I was reminded by my son that it needed to be made—before Christmas. I opened the surprise package, and out bounced candy canes, bright-red gumdrops, and fanciful lollipops. Actually, that's what

Hairy Leg News

I wanted to come out. What really cascaded from the box were ugly, round, hard candies, dull black-and-beige gumdrops, and no red candies. My son was excited that we were going to get candies and cookies and have fun. He might even get to lick the spoon.

I started the assembly with my four-year-old slithering down the sofa in a laundry basket. He would be doing the gingerbread house under "observer status," at least until decorating. My other son, a bit older, helped to cut the squares. We placed them in the oven and then set them out to cool.

Next came the icing. Not one to read instructions, I let the icing sit hardening under a damp towel. Then I slapped on the glue-like substance like concrete. If we were really lucky, the gumdrops would not wander off, and the chimney would not crash down into the house. "Prepare frosting one pouch at a time" danced in our heads. We slathered the globby icing and stuck seven little gingerbread men outside the front door, which we did not open for fear it would fall; instead it was a cutout, attached at one side.

We positioned evergreen trees like toy soldiers around the house with candy hearts, which I had run back to the store to purchase. The rooftops glistened with ho-hum beige-and-brown gumdrops. It was about this time that I noticed the roof on the left side become an avalanche. Then the back wall buckled. "Mom, the house is falling!"

"Don't worry, son, we have a plan B." I grabbed the back of the house, which snapped in my hand. We were in dire need of home repairs. I disassembled the entire house and cut one of the rooftops in two. Now, instead of an A-frame roof, we had a Caribbean fiesta model. I let the two roof pieces hang over the sidewalls, the way you build a house of cards. Not bad. In the gingerbread architect awards for innovation, it may have rated a B.

My son said the stars were pillows, and the house was a bed. Then the stars turned into angels and flew to the other side of the bed.

"There, now it looks like a church," I declared. We hoped the icing would hold. And it did. That stuff hardened even more, and there would be no prying off any gumdrop.

Halloween Potluck

Announcement: The company's social committee is celebrating Halloween with a potluck. The potluck will be a *green* potluck, so please bring your own plate and cutlery if you can. Upon reading this ad for a company Halloween potluck, I thought the food had to be green—like green Jell-O, guacamole, or green-dyed cookies. I also thought the company was being a frugalmeister for making us bring our own plates and forks.

Stolen Halloween Candy

I heard on the news that a grown man in Yellowknife had stolen an eight-year-old's Halloween candy and that the local radio station is collecting extra candy for this child. I asked my husband what he was doing Halloween night in that Godzilla mask!

Her Majesty's Visit at Halloween

Recently we had about fifty kids stumble up to our front door for Halloween, so it was a good thing that we had lots of candy. The warmer weather brought them out in full force. In fine northern tradition, they wore their costumes over their parkas. One frail, wispy girl about aged five came up to the door with her parents lagging behind on the stairs below. She looked shy. I said, "Oh, you must be a princess!" She went in a pissed-off, strong voice, "*No!* Everyone keeps calling me a princess. I'm *not* a princess. I'm a *queen!*" I said, "Oh, OK, Your Majesty, here's your candy." It was priceless. Her parents were snickering as I'm sure they'd heard her say that all night long. Other visitors included some skeletons, robots, a mad scientist costume that was a hoot, witches good and bad, and a couple of Batmans who had apparently cloned themselves. There were a few cardboard-box costumes, which are always a hoot as you see them trying to squeeze into the front door to get their candy. There were no nursery-rhyme characters at all and definitely no ghosts. It is not like the costumes we had as kids. Back then most kids wore white sheets with holes cut out for the eyes, which moved too much to see your way up and down stairs. By the end of the night, some ghosts were wearing their eyes on the backs of their heads. The masks were hard to breathe through and made our faces sweaty or fogged up our eyeglasses. When the elastic straps snapped, they would zing into our chins, leaving a red welt.

Neighbor's Halloween Decorations

My neighbor's favorite time of year is Halloween. Sally has her house fully decorated with Halloween stuff. Gauze ghosts and flying witches hang over her doorstep. Her front yard is done up as a graveyard with crosses and gravestones bordered by fake police barrier tape. It's like living across from the Macy's window decorator. I love my neighbor, and we all tease her about it every year. She's the first one to have her decorations up, and they are the most creative in town.

Halloween Visitors

Sally and her friend came over for five minutes so we could see their costumes. She was dressed as Alice in Wonderland,

and my hubby had to explain the story to me as I had no clue. When I was younger, we had Mother Goose stories and Hans Christian Anderson stories, and I never was told the tale of Alice in Wonderland. Anyway, he looked at me like I had three heads because I didn't know the story.

I grew up in a very private Italian family, with limited knowledge of stuff like that. My grandfather and mother's first languages were Italian and French and then English. On my father's side, German was their first language. However, I do know how to peel a grape and make homemade lasagna.

Halloween Getaway

My son reminded me of the time I drove him and two friends to the other end of town to trick-or-treat where the houses are closer together—the strategy being to collect more Halloween candy. I waited in the car as they ran from house to house. When their bags filled up, they would come to the car, empty their bags, and go back for more. It was like I was driving the getaway car. And the driver got her cut of the candy. When they were finished, we drove off, candy-bar wrappers flying into the backseat.

Fred's Bar

There was a note on my windshield after work. I was thinking, *Did I park too close to the guy behind me, or are they plowing the streets?* The note under the wiper blade read, "Love is sometimes irritable, so this Valentine's Day enjoy an eight-course meal for only eighty dollars a couple at Fred's Bar." It's a grabber.

In the News: Typical Canadian News Stories

Canadian news stories are like no others. They may involve the weather, hockey, politicians, or maple syrup. Other hot topics are snow and the weather, more snow, and the end of snow.

Ten

PARENTING IN EXTREME CLIMATES

Drive Me Here, Drive Me There

When my kids were little, I was constantly in and out of the driveway taking them somewhere. We should have had orange pylons at the end to indicate this driveway was really a thruway. We came up with a little rhyme to reflect this: "Drive me here, drive me there, drive me in your underwear." It was like being a Daytona driver, pulling into the pit stop, hitting the brakes, and careening into the driveway. The kids ran inside, emptied their backpacks of school tools, refilled them with games, and it was on to the next house with the stopwatch ticking.

One time, I started backing out of the driveway and heard the urgent appeal of "Mom, stop!" Hitting the brakes, I noticed that a friend of theirs was hanging off the rear door.

I was also known to go to drive-thru establishments in my nightgown and comfy housecoat in quest of early-morning coffee, hoping that no policeman would pull me over as I always needed to get home to drive the kids somewhere. I half convinced myself that this wardrobe fit in with the trend of kids wearing pajama bottoms to high school.

Pop-Can Incident

I dropped my son off at work, and, as soon as the car started again, there was a rattling noise like my engine was coming apart in pieces. It was -37°C that day. Maybe it needed oil. Should we stop at the repair shop and get them to test drive it, or take the chance and run home with it like that? As I started driving faster, the rattling noise got worse. My seatbelt was half off me, and I was thinking my car was going to blow up and that I'd better be prepared to ditch it. I drove all the way home with this rattling noise, looking in my rearview mirror for parts falling off and thinking, yes, maybe it's time for a trade-in. It was only after pulling into the driveway that my son's pop can rattling in the drink holder came into my view. The cold weather and snow had amplified the sound.

On Kids Being Locked Out of the House

My friend's daughter is standing on top of their camper in -10°C talking on her cell phone. Obviously, she's been locked out of the house and gave up trying to haul herself over the second-floor railing to the sun deck in her heavy boots and parka.

My sons were continually locking themselves out of the house before cell phones were invented. One time a neighbor helped one of them break in. Other times they went to a neighbor's place to warm up. There they were treated with all kinds of hot food, superior Xbox entertainment, and friendly pets. After such a smorgasbord of afterschool hospitality, I thought they might never come home, but they eventually did grudgingly return.

Music Lessons

My son was taking school music lessons, and he and two of his friends wanted to learn the easiest instrument. They chose the baritone, a mini tuba, which normally has four buttons. Their instruments, however, were short a button, so they had to learn only the A, B, and C notes. It was not a career choice.

In a Gadda da Vida, Baby!

We always try to teach our sons about music from bygone decades. We were sitting in the car waiting for my son's friend, who we were picking up, when Iron Butterfly's "In a Gadda da Vida" came in loud on my car's stereo.

I asked my son if he'd ever heard the drum solo song before as it's classic psychedelic rock from 1968. Long pause. Yes, he had heard it before. I'm thinking, *Wow, I've really educated my son in old songs—success at last!* He then tells me the song was on an episode of *The Simpsons*, pulls out his cell phone, and shows me the exact spot in the episode. It's the "Bart Sells His Soul" episode, where the family is in church, and Bart has doctored the hymnals so that the parishioners have the music to "In a Gadda da Vida" instead. At the end of the very long song, the exhausted organist collapses in a heap. So now I'm deflated, thinking the Simpsons are teaching my son music history, not me. Ay-yi-yi!

When I got back home, I listened to the original full version on the Internet—all seventeen minutes and three seconds (bandwidth, shmandwidth). In the old days, the song took up the entire second side of a record album. That was quite an accomplishment.

There have been many comments about this song. It is a psychedelic monument, and rockers would still love to know what it means. It has also been stated that originally the acid-rock song was supposed to be called "In the Garden of Eden," but the words somehow got slurred, and "In a Gadda Da Vida" sounded good, so they left it that way. To me it is classic rock of the 1960s, and its history should be passed on to future generations. It marks a time when psychedelic music started to form heavy metal. The song is ranked the twenty-fourth greatest hard rock song of all time by VH1, according to Wikipedia.

Attention

If you want to get your husband's or kid's attention, just try sitting on the couch eating bonbons, reading a magazine, and looking content.

Can I Get a Ride?

Upon walking in the door after a hard day at work, I was typically greeted with "Can we get a ride?" This usually involved driving one of my children through a whiteout-, blizzard-, or gale-warning day to the far end of town. On nice-weather days, they chose to stay home. It appeared that all of my sons had friends who lived at the other end of town, not one in our neighborhood. The upshot of that was chauffeuring them for twenty-six years while they were growing up. This makes a parent adept at running out in the evening in a nightgown, fuzzy pink slippers, and a bathrobe under a nice warm parka—and hoping to God no policeman pulled the car over for any reason.

In the Kitchen, Belly Itching

Cooking for a family of five when the kids were all home, I had my share of kitchen disasters. There were one-clump onion rings, exploding ravioli, sparking angel food cake, and arcing foil-wrapped bacon in the microwave. Other times when I've been forgetful, I've conjured up translucent coffee, chicken with gizzards still in the cavity, and a flaming birthday cake in the oven where the chocolate oozed over the sides like lava. My latest foray into the dark crevasses of our kitchen was to make banana loaf. Sounds easy. It came out like a rock. It was so tough I dropkicked it out the front door and into the snowbank below. I have found great salvation in frozen pizzas, oven-ready chicken fingers, and hot dogs.

Mornings

People who know me well know I need serious coffee before starting a conversation in the morning. My morning vocabulary is "huh?"

Mornings are the golden opportunity to discover there are no more clean socks, towels, or face cloths. School cash is required for Dr. Seuss productions, bus money, and swimming pool money. The wallet remnants—zipper askew, drivers' license and change cascading out—is all that is left after the book club, picture taking, and excursions have exhausted its contents. My purse had been discarded or dropkicked into a corner on its noggin.

Morning of False Starts

You have never seen upheaval in the morning until you have seen a family sleep in, discover there is no bread for sandwiches, and they have five minutes to make it to school. Running out of juice boxes or snacks would send us into a tizzy.

When we got to school, one son did not have a warm enough coat. So I drove backward for a block and let him retrieve a warmer parka. I think of the serenity after dropping them off, only realizing at dismissal time I get to do it all again only in reverse when they forget their notes, backpacks, book orders, or bag of carrots.

School Notes

The most favorite notes our kids forget are usually about school closures, parent-teacher interviews, séances, and professional development days. Their next favorite notes to forget are about needles and parental permissions. They handily give you invitations to school functions the morning of the events, unless, of course, it is after the event. You need 3-D glasses to peer at the notes through the tomato-squished topography.

We would get newsletters with regularity because the students could win a draw prize if they returned the back page with their parents' signature. Smart thinking.

Jell-O and red juice congealed on notes were de rigueur. Add to that a wet bathing suit so it would then be a gelled, leaking note. I personally vote for schools sending e-mailed notes. Sticking your hand in backpacks would not be as jolting. And you might actually get to see school events.

Sandwich making for kids is a serious art form. My childhood sandwiches were the five-day creative use of jumbled assortments of peanut butter variations: peanut butter and banana; no peanut butter, just jam; honey, cinnamon, marmalade; or more peanut butter. Nowadays, kids have sandwiches with no nuts in them.

On the return run from school, the kids would bring back the not-eaten tomato sandwiches, which someone obviously sat on or stepped on. They slid out of the lunch bag into the backpack innards. The orange juice dripping from a plastic bottle smelled vile. You held the school note fetched from the backpack between your thumb and index finger and proclaimed, "Oh, you get out early on Friday."

Sally's Young Son Gets a Needle

Of course, with winter comes flu season. I did a repeated favor for Sally and took her son Jack for his not-so-annual flu shot since she could not leave work that day. He had an irrational fear of needles, and the last time he'd had a hysterical fit and ran out of the building. To anyone walking into the building, it looked like he had discovered some big-eyed stick bug caught between his T-shirt and his belly button. So I thought, *OK, kid, we're lining up yet again at the multiplex for God knows how long. And I may have to give him the needle myself.*

In the line outside the multiplex, he was talking with some high-school students who were smoking yellow herbal cigarettes with ginseng. The other told me that before we got there, two individuals who had fainted were carried out on stretchers by the ambulance EMTs. I said, "Oh, I won't tell Sally's son about that until well after his needle."

So her son was now holding up the number sixty-nine, which he turned upside down so it read ninety-six, as in Big Chicken. When they called his number, I went up with him, and he sat down, looked the other way, and got the needle, no fuss, no nothing. What was that? Well, according to him, he had seen some friends on the way in who said it didn't hurt at all, and he felt that he had to act tough for the other kids. Then, when we got home, it turned out that Sally's husband had bribed her son with twenty dollars to get his needle, and after that they took him for pizza. Who knew?

Jack the Cashier

Sally's son Jack's first job was working as a grocery-store cashier. When he first started working, he rolled the oranges and lemons down the conveyor belt after entering their prices on the register. I guess ten years of bowling lessons finally paid off. He also had to learn how to handle grumpy customers. I told him not to take it personally. He told a customer that the turnip the guy was buying could clobber someone over the head pretty good. Remarkably, he is still working there.

On Being Distracted

Sally, who normally picks up her children from daycare or school in a certain order, decided to reverse the order one day. She thought her last pickup child was lost, so she called the police. She had forgotten that she had dropped him off somewhere after picking him up. Sally sat in her vehicle just staring.

Being distracted with kids is not unusual. One time Sally was backing up out of her driveway with the radio up full and the kids yacking in the back seat. She heard a crash and realized a bus just took off her back bumper and part of her trunk. She stopped, got out of the car, and tossed her trunk lid into the snowbank. She pulled back into her driveway and phoned into work that she would not be in that day.

While being distracted by my own kids, I have flattened five garbage cans, boiled rice with no rice in the pot, and put my clothes on inside out, or, as my son calls it, "inside in and outside out."

When I try to watch TV, I am asked, "Mom, what's that?" "Mom, why is he going there?" "Mom, do you have a Loonie aka Canadian dollar?" "Mom, I don't want to look." "Mom, come see this." It is much easier to wait until they're in bed. Kid distraction tactics happen at the best times: when you're on a long-distance call, sojourning in the bathtub, reading *War and Peace*, hanging drapes, or putting up weather stripping. Other times are while painting a room, counting knitting stitches, or trying to cram for an accounting test.

Kids also distract themselves. Once my son forgot his camping money for cubs and raced back to the van. He ran smack into the outside van mirror and gave himself a headache.

Adults distract their kids by making them do chores, reminding them to do chores, and commenting on why the chores are not done. They also have a habit of postponing fun events until the chores are completed.

Traveling South with Arctic-Bred Children

When northerners travel south with children who've been raised in the Arctic, there are some surprises. Sally's son

Jack thought he saw an observatory when they were in the south. "Uh, no, son, that's a silo." He had never seen manhole covers before we went south. In Inuvik, due to permafrost, the sewage travels through utilidors, which carry water, and sewer pipes above ground. The pipes are covered by corrugated steel. Sally's son used to peer down the manhole covers looking for moving objects. He had never seen real green grass until they were south as Inuvik back then did not have landscaping. The kids loved running barefoot through grass in the south in the rain. Their first time swimming in southern ocean waves Sally had to teach them to turn around so that the waves wouldn't hit them in the face. They also discovered there was more variety of birds and dogs than just ravens and Huskies.

Story Something

Coming from a large Italian family, I found it was nothing for twenty-nine of us to go together to a theme park for kids. One day we took our kids to Story Something as I can never remember the name of the park. It started to rain. The Story Something party of twenty-nine started speeding with strollers and kids toward the exit. This was at the other end of the park. Some forty-five minutes later, after a stop for a diaper change, we ran to our vehicles. Amazingly we all made it to the parking lot in one vast swoop and we were still all together in one big moving unit.

Arctic Recess in the Dark

Located in the Western Arctic Region, Inuvik has fifty-six days a year of twenty-four-hour sunlight. In winter, there are more than thirty days of continual twenty-four-hour darkness. My first observation when I arrived there was that kids were having their recess time outside in the dark. That struck me as odd. During the summer months, it was a standing joke that we wouldn't tell our kids to come home when it gets dark like we heard when we were growing up. People who have lived there for long periods enjoy really long summers as a result. For example, you can go fishing at two in the morning in summertime daylight.

Happy "Others'" Day

Raising boys, I have grown accustomed to BB guns, which are normally played with outside the house. However, one day I came home and found that the plastic sign in my flowers displayed not "Happy Mothers' Day" but "Happy others' Day." Yes, indeed, a BB gun pellet had taken out the M. I have kept it as a reminder of my motherhood and my children's childhood.

Top Pet Peeves of Working Mothers

- No suitable fake furs or real diamonds on sale at the local box store to wear to work.

- "You want it when?" This has been replaced by "You mean layoff, pay rollback, or job redundancy?"
- No wardrobes fitting childbearing women, just models.
- No leisure time to pursue hobbies of earthworm collecting and darning plant hangers.
- Time-management and organizational skills of raising a family count for zilch.
- After decades in the workforce, you realize teenagers make more than you do.
- Job security means going for coffee break and still having a desk when you come back.
- Being an optimist means taking your lunch to work.
- You have a house full of sick kids and you are sick too. The only video rentals available are *The Lost Weekend*, *The Blob*, and *Eight for Eggrolls*.
- You have figured out a way to juggle career and motherhood. The answer is a part-time job. The first day on the job you discover your new desk is located in the hallway next to the elevator. The first moment of free time after childbirth you decide to make the most of your time by listening to a telemarketer at suppertime, phoning income tax and being put on hold, and trying to decipher the mathematical equation for the milk-to-cereal ratio so there is no milk left in the bowl when the cereal is eaten.
- Your husband and kids keep saying, "Just come here and see this." Your answer is to hide under a bed,

pretend you left the house, bang the front door, and then come in the back door and sneak downstairs to hide in your office.

- After leaving work at 5:30 p.m., you pick up your kids, go home, and start supper for four cranky, hungry people clutching your ankles. It's time to break out wieners on sticks, give them something healthy like pizza roll-ups, or give them a soup and sandwich, which they will tell you is the same as what they had at school or work.

- You have moved to a new town and are only using a transitional wardrobe of bowling socks, stretchy pants, and T-shirts. Your kids have one good change of clothes. This is a good indicator that your new washing machine will break down as soon as you turn the knob, which comes off in your hand, or the kids have outgrown their clothes on the two-hour flight to your new home.

Tips for Helping Your Teenager Pick a College or University

Choosing a college or university for your teenager can be exciting and stressful at the same time. Here are some things to look for when helping your teenager pick a college or university:

- Shoparama is right across the street.
- There are only five-star hotels and gourmet restaurants in the area.

- The average yearly temperature is above 80°F.
- There's something in it for you, the parent, such as a nearby casino and hobby shop.
- The residence rooms are bigger than a breadbox.
- The floor monitor hasn't stolen your son or daughter's room because it has the best view of the lake and mountains.
- There is an orientation barbecue that offers all you can eat hamburgers until you have time to do your first grocery order for the first semester.
- There are five burger joints, a liquor store, and three grocery stores all within walking distance of the residence.
- The entire volleyball team, football team, and basketball team greet you at the residence entrance to help take all your belongings up to your tenth-floor room via the elevator or stairs.
- The extracurricular activities include free tennis and golf lessons.
- There is a pinball arcade within walking distance.
- The residence room comes with a toaster oven.
- The curriculum is full of lightweight courses such as how to transpose harpsichord scores for trombones, how to make balloon animals, and how to build a kiosk for the sale of old school books. Other optional courses would be how to water a plant with a

Hairy Leg News

shot glass, how to hang clothes from a treadmill, and how to avoid hockey, football, and baseball games by adjusting the television set so that it looks like it is broken.

Eleven

AGING IN THE NORTH

Beauty Cream Delivery

It is great that we have super mailboxes in the cul-de-sac. However, there is a downside to that perk. For example, when you receive a free sample of some beauty cream, and the cream is a solid chunk that has been sitting in the super mailbox in -40°C for quite some time. According to the label, the cream fights the many signs of aging. It claims to minimize the appearance of pores. Maybe I should just scotch tape the whole frozen sample pack to my forehead.

Sally's Cell Phone

Sally received a phone call while she was cooking and misplaced her cell phone. Dinner was served, and when it was all cleared up, she started looking for her cell phone. She called it from her landline and heard her fridge ringing. She opened the fridge door and found her cell phone inside beside the pastrami. The same day she also forgot where she had parked. Could this be the onset of menopause?

Middle-Aged Party

I attended my neighbor Sally's "middle-aged party," where we all fell asleep on couches by 9:00 p.m. watching TV after eating a vat of cheese she brought back from Costco—aged cheddar, yummy and accompanied by white iced wine.

The warmth of her rabbit-pellet stove and her small, fluffy pet dog snuggling at my feet knocked me out as I relaxed on her couch. I woke up at 11:30 p.m., let myself out her back door, and crawled home. Next time, we'll aim for something really daring like staying up until midnight.

Weird Dreams

I had one of the weirdest dreams the other night. The heroine in my dream tried to hitch a ride with the Muppets on a motorized toy car in an amusement park, but it had already left with her brother, son, and two Muppets. She was looking around the pub for someone. She then left and got lost in an American city. She walked through a front door and down the sidewalk and saw David from *Coronation Street* in a brawl but managed to sidestep the fight. I blame this dream on the smoked cheddar cheese we ate at the middle-aged party.

Liberation 95

There has been a lot of talk about Liberation 95. As baby boomers approach retirement, there are lots of financial plans targeted at this age group. It's commonly accepted that many baby boomers could be retiring before age 65 with the financial freedom to do so. In my opinion, this is a goal that very few of us could realistically achieve. The stock market dips, and dismal financial market events globally put the kibosh on that dream for many boomers. The fiscal cliff was another clue that retirement was not around the corner. The mental image of working at age ninety-five is not a pretty sight.

Semiretirement

This morning, while I was outside having a coffee and deadheading my hanging baskets, my son was talking to me through the screen door about some clown song. As a man with a dog walked by, I commented to my son, "Yeah, what movie was that from?" But my son had gone downstairs. The man walking the dog I'm sure thinks I was talking to myself or to the plants. Perfect!

This is week two of semiretirement.

Choosing a Retirement Community

Many people my age are looking for retirement communities. For some northerners, that means staying put. For others who cannot afford to live in Yellowknife, they look to the south and plan their house hunt and ultimate move or, in some cases, *ultimate removal* as it is called up here.

One retirement area I saw online had a tornado warning for today. The very next story—about a lakefront property we had been looking at—reported that dead whitefish were washing up on shore. A scientist said the heat was depriving the lake of oxygen, resulting in all these dead fish. Strike that one from the list.

The other retirement places we're looking at have the potential for earthquakes, volcanoes, wildfires, and hurricanes. I guess it all goes with the yin and yang of hot climates. So, for now, I'm considering retirement in a non-coastal, non-hurricane, non-flooding area. I guess that means we're staying where we are in the frozen North—or Phoenix, Arizona, sounds good.

Tips for Middle Age

Entering middle age is not for the meek. There are physical and psychological changes that can affect people in middle age. Here are some tips on surviving middle age:

- As Dustin Hoffman has been credited with stating, and I am loosely paraphrasing, "Never give up a chance to go to the bathroom." Tip: know where every bathroom is located in shopping malls.

- Be prepared for batwings, gray thinning hair, and no patience. Tip: go for long drives to forget all this by focusing on nature.

- Gray hairs are appearing everywhere. Tip: always have your hair stylist on speed dial for gray root cover-ups.

- Chin hairs are growing like weeds. Tip: learn to appreciate and enjoy your Frank Sinatra and Dean Martin music while plucking chin hairs.

- One of the first signs of middle age is when the skin on your face starts resembling a saddlebag. Tip: pay a little extra and get the deep-cell-reaching, linebacker-strength creams.

- Your consumption of alcohol rises as does your blood pressure. Tip: get a good bartender guidebook and go for walks in nature.

- You start to see patterns more often, such as, "Oh, it's only another seven months before we have to put up another Christmas tree!" You also start paying more attention to the calendar. Tip: get a really nice calendar.

- You realize that you don't fit those pants anymore, and it's not because you shrank them in the laundry. Your belly, which used to sit right below your boobs, has suddenly slid like a bag of cement down to your belly

Hairy Leg News

button. In fact, your entire body shape has changed, and you have become pear-shaped. Your first thought is that gravity has increased on earth because it could not possibly be a lifestyle thing. Tip: wear loose-fitting clothes and buy a larger size or shop in the men's section for big T-shirts at half the price.

- Cravings for sweets have risen dramatically, and passing donut shops is getting harder and harder. Tip: start making homemade donuts.

- Recognize that there is a brain fog that comes with middle age. You go through the drive-thru, pay for your order, and drive right past the pickup window, forgetting your order. This would never have happened when you were seventeen years old. Tip: order at the inside counter.

- You start writing down passwords, whereas before you just muddled your way through. Tip: keep a logbook of passwords.

- Eating healthier has moved to the top of your food purchase list, and snack foods have slithered to the bottom of the list like a snakes-and-ladders game. You still buy snack foods but not as many, and the healthy foods sit at the bottom of your fridge, decomposing before you ever get to them. Tip: eat the healthy foods first.

- You start eyeing the world map more closely to form a bucket list of trips you would still like to take before you pop your clogs. Tip: get a good laminated map for your wall.

- If James Bond walked into your home, you'd tell him, "Not now. I have to pluck my chin hairs." Your couch time has increased exponentially to your fatigue factor, and you whine about it more. Tip: pick up a new hobby or interest.

- A tendency to swear has ramped up due to an increasing lack of patience especially when behind the wheel of a car. Tip: take the back roads whenever possible. It may cost more in gas, but it makes driving a lot more tolerable. Crank up the tunes and bring your cell phone in case you get lost.

- Your empathy levels decrease. You have no time for anything. Tip: read a good book on how to restore empathy levels. Or better yet—who cares?

- You start wishing for practical gifts, whereas in your youth you hoped for fun gifts. Tip: buy yourself a fun gift such as a computer game.

- You start noticing that there are still tags on the dish towels that you bought and have used a million times. Same for the pillows in the bedroom. Before you were too busy living your life to notice, or if you did notice, you didn't care. Tip: you have way too much time on your hands, so get a part-time job, take a dog-grooming course, or visit a friend.

Hairy Leg News

- Makeup just accentuates your wrinkles. Tip: go au naturel or get a good headband that appears to give you a mini facelift. Research the new nonsurgical ultrasoundlike facelift.
- With the onset of menopause, you become grumpy and bitchy. Tip: develop new words to describe these moods, such as *gritchy*.
- When you have hot flashes in a cold climate, you can run outside and jump into a snowbank to cool down.
- You receive a bill for a rectal exam from the dentist. Tip: put on your reading glasses; it's actually a "recall" exam.

Writing-a-Book Avoidance

There are many ways to avoid having to sit down to write a book. These distractions vary from day-to-day. Here are some of the more frequent ones:

- Deck sitting
- Excessive vacuuming
- Excessive cleaning and decluttering
- Researching the three *M*s: mold, mildew, and mothballs
- Finding five thousand uses for dishcloths
- Reading other books and certainly not your own
- Refilling empty juice containers

- Rejigging shish kebob skewers as sewing-machine thread holders
- Enjoying the distraction of power outages
- Warming lip wax on the stove and dealing with the aftermath—wax fumes intermingling with your sautéed mushrooms—and finding ways to eliminate the odors
- Baking a cake for your family and then baking another for a potluck
- Answering the phone, door, and intercom buzzers
- Putting up notes on the fridge indicating foods you like—but not expecting your family to like them
- Doing some creative math: how many meals have I made each day for twenty-eight years? (3 meals/day x 365 days/year x 28 years—or approximately thirty thousand meals)
- More creative math: how many haircuts has my hairstylist friend given? (30 years x multitudinous cuts = 78,000 haircuts)
- Researching refrigerators—then and now
- Taking all the glassware out of the china cabinet, hand washing it, and then placing it all back into the cabinet
- Cutting off mattress, towel, and pillow tags
- Putting gummy bears in the microwave
- Coming up with ring-around-the-tub solutions

Hairy Leg News

- Trying to remove red-dye stains from the white shag carpet
- Understanding tactics of family members for pet-care avoidance
- Understanding how to trace clues of who left snow footprints all over the house and how to do forensic sole matching
- Searching out eye drops for dry eyes
- Checking the broiler setting while cooking bacon and then fanning smoke with beach towels or newspapers and opening doors in -40°C to clear the smoke while watching the baby cry and holding his ears as the smoke detector goes off
- Catching up on *Coronation Street* episodes
- Learning how to cook by watching food shows on television
- Watching two back-to-back CFL football games
- Becoming a new, instant fan of the Toronto Blue Jays—"Go, Jays!"
- Researching all you want to know about lead (It is used in the batteries of cars, forklifts, and baggage carts; for soldering with tin; as a sound barrier in buildings; in shields for X-ray equipment; and in primer for painting iron and steel.)
- Cleaning out the fridge and freezer
- Talking with the neighbor over the fence

- Getting a pad of sticky notes, writing notes to yourself, and posting them all over your computer, in your desk, and on the telephone, ceiling, and in-tray
- Deciding your computer screen is too dusty, grabbing a rag, and starting cleaning—then realizing your keyboard and the rest of the house are dusty, too, and proceeding to clean the house
- Looking up at your framed photos, deciding you don't like the frames, taking them all apart, moving photos around, and placing them back in frames; next discovering the tiny nails will not stay in their holes anymore and proceeding to get a rather large hammer and pound them; discovering glass shattering and walking to a box store to get more frames
- Seeing a dirt spot on your wall and deciding to wash it and then deciding that won't be enough and proceeding to repaint the room
- Deciding you don't know enough about your family's heritage and calling up your Aunt Edith; starting from scratch and creating a family tree; mailing it to all your relatives
- Noticing you do not have enough lighting on your computer; standing on a chair to redirect the track lighting; returning to the computer with spots before your eyes

Hairy Leg News

- Spending time making a psychedelic sign for your home office door: "Caution, menopausal woman writer at work. Do not enter!"

That is my hairy-leg news. And now back to more snow shoveling.

Made in the USA
Charleston, SC
18 May 2016